The author is an Irish female with a passion for writing. She has been writing for years, including fiction and poetry. She is married to Declan and comes from a very family-orientated background, loves the outdoors, walking by the sea with her German Shepherd cross, Jaz. She lives in Galway, in the heart of the Claddagh.

I would like to dedicate my book to the memory of my mother, Phil.

A beautiful heart. After the loss of whom, I thought my heart would never heal.

This is for you, Mam.

Mary Finnerty-Morris

One Chance

Austin Macauley Publishers™

LONDON • CAMBRIDGE • NEW YORK • SHARJAH

A CIP catalogue record for this title is available from the British Library.

ISBN 9781528900997 (Paperback)
ISBN 9781528901000 (Hardback)
ISBN 9781528901017 (Kindle e-book)
ISBN 9781528956956 (ePub e-book)

www.austinmacauley.com

First Published (2019)
Austin Macauley Publishers Ltd
25 Canada Square
Canary Wharf
London
E14 5LQ

Chapter One

It was early morning. June sighed gently as she strolled along the beach. Two days never the same, today a soft ripple at the water's edge brought her back to her childhood days; endless days of sunshine (it seemed).

Could she have taken a different road in life, or is life mapped out for everyone? Are we as a feather blowing in the wind of fate having little or no power over our final destination?

Who knows?

"You're out early," a familiar voice brought her back from her almost dazed state. It was old Walter, now retired from his fishing days, he liked to potter around on the pier, chat with the lads and tie up their ropes for them, exhausted after their early morning trip to the deep for their catch.

Not an easy life, but for most around these parts, a way of life that was in their blood. *Must be a great sense of freedom,* June thought, heading off into the blue.

She'd greeted the old man with her usual warm smile. Dear old Walter, who had given her many a shoulder to cry on. Living in a small fishing village was easy, somewhat safe. Having had opportunities to move on and choosing to stay, June now wondered and spent many a waking moment wondering, had she chosen well?

What if she had chosen to go with Matt to make a life in America, where would she be now, would she be happy?

So many ifs! So many regrets!

Now she would never know. One thing she did know, however, life gives you 'one chance'!

Had she not forgotten to get the eggs in the supermarket that day (so long ago now), she would never have met Matt.

Probably be content to be settled with a nice local lad, of which there were many.

"Don't forget to check the date," June passing herself out in her usual hurried state, reached for the eggs (a fairly vital ingredient for tea on pancake Tuesday), how she had forgotten them earlier on in the weekly shop, she'll never know!

But then she thought to herself, *You were born forgetful my dear, your head will never save your legs.*

A stranger smiled at her, a rare thing in these parts, for one to meet a stranger in the local shop.

"That one has his money made," her nan would say, "three prices on everything." It was miles to the nearest big store and most not with their own transport.

June smiled back.

"Sure you'd melt the heart of any man, giving smiles away like they were ten a penny," Pop would say as he tousled her hair, dear Pop. The good old days, life was simple then, no confusion, just your nan and your pop and your daily chores.

June's mam, it seemed, got caught up in some sort of bother years since and had taken off for herself, leaving her daughter 'a raw infant' as Nan would say, to be reared on nothing. There was nothing yet there was everything.

"Hi, I'm Matt," a stranger, but only for a moment.

Within exchanging a few words, June felt she had known Matt all her life. He was sort of—comfortable to talk to.

Maybe that is who your soul mate is, someone you've not yet met and when you do, you recognise each other!

Chapter Two

He would be around for a while, had his boat tied up for the bad weather, they would probably bump into each other again, and so they did.

In fact, Matt made it his business, it seems, to run out of milk or something almost every time June went to the corner shop. Became a bit embarrassing after a while! Then he asked her out for a drink in the pub by the quay.

Sure, what was the harm in that! No harm at all, if it hadn't shaped the rest of her life!

The evening went well, Nan was so glad to see June walking out with 'a nice young fella', spent far too much time in the ashes, she had thought.

Matt was twenty-four, two years younger than June, they had often joked about it. He would say he didn't mind her being the elder lemon, he liked his women mature!

They would giggle and kiss!

At what point, did those friendly kisses grow into so much more! So much that she yearned for the next one!

This was stuff for storybooks, June had read many of her nan's old love storybooks. She could lose herself in one of those stories, snuggled up on Pop's old chair for the night.

"Best not be reading too much into that stuff," Nan used to say, "fill your head with notions."

That's rich! June thought, coming from the one with a whole chest full of them!

Wasn't hard coming back to reality then, you only had to put the book down. However, when reality puts you into another world, there is no escaping it, and June didn't want to escape it either! This was the happiest time of her life.

In Matt's arms, she felt like someone else, she was finding herself. Finding new feelings she had never experienced before, feelings she never knew existed. Sure, she'd felt safe and loved with her nan and pop, and she'd had the odd crush on one or two of the local lads growing up. But this was different.

"Best not be sitting there too long in the cold, there's a storm a brewing," old Walter shouted from the pier. Boats all tied up, he was heading for shelter.

June was sitting at the water's edge, it didn't seem cold to her.

The memories of that day, a few years since now, were keeping her warm.

'Matt loves June' was the inscription on the quay wall.

He'd written it from the boat while bobbing around in the water like a cork. A storm had been brewing that day too, only it wasn't affecting the weather!

Matt would soon be on his way, the weather had settled.

There was no danger now, no reason for him not to go.

They'd had many good times, and had become became close, too close probably! Soon the waters that had brought them together would divide them.

"Want to come sailing with me tomorrow?" Matt was halfway down the garden path when he shouted back. "Weather's looking good!"

"Ya, okay." June wasn't a fan of the sea but she would go, she would be fine. She locked up, didn't really fancy hot chocolate tonight. She'd go straight to bed. Hadn't been sleeping so good these past few nights.

Not much sleep on her now either. Matt hadn't said anything but she'd felt there was something he had wanted to say.

Was he taking her sailing for a reason? Was he soon to be on his way? He would break it to her gently.

Chapter Three

Just like Matt to be so considerate, she was going to miss him. However, she must not tell him that, he must not have the slightest idea that she'd be heartbroken after him.

Matt had his plans, she was not going to get in the way of him pursuing them!

With fair winds in her sails, he proudly took the 'Mary Ellen' out in the bay. Full steam ahead till they passed the lighthouse. Hardly a ripple now, it was amazing. So peaceful. They lay watching the gentle breeze play the sails, floating along to the whisper of the sea.

"June," her heart sank. *This is it*, she thought, *he'll soon be on his way.*

"After a lot of thought, I've decided to sell the 'Mary Ellen'." June looked up. *What was he saying? Was he going to stay?*

Had her sleepless nights been in vain?

However, her relief was short lived.

"I'm going further afield, going to America." Mouth open, June glared speechless as he continued, "And I want you to come with me."

He moved closer and held her, so tight she gasped for breath.

"I love you June—I know we haven't known each other for long, but I do know I want to be with you, I want to show you the world."

At that moment, in his strong embrace, June could have agreed to anything. She knew in her heart she had fallen for Matt the first day ever.

She hadn't expected this, how could she up and leave and go to America?

She couldn't.

Matt was independent, and she'd seen that in the way he'd looked at life. He'd broken his ties with his family long since, kept in touch of course but had made his own way.

June had Nan to think about, and now since Pop had passed on she depended on her even more. She couldn't up and leave!

It would break Nan's heart to see her go, it was going to break June's heart to stay!

"I'm sorry June, I thought—" Matt started up the engine, they headed for home. Clouds seemed to gather, blocking the sun. June sat calmly hiding the tears. As they approached the quay wall, the engine was turned off.

They would sail in on the breeze, prolonging the agony.

June couldn't wait to get her feet on the pier, she wanted to run, scream, get away from this deafening silence.

Then Matt pulled in alongside the quay wall and started to inscribe their names on the wall.

There was only so long she could hold back the tears!

Matt held her close, as if he had heard her heart breaking, for what could only have been minutes but seemed like an eternity.

"Nice day for it," Walter was waiting to tie up the ropes. Matt was a likable sort had fitted in around here like it was in his blood. But it wasn't, soon the ties would be broken.

June was aching!

They walked hand in hand, as they had done so many times before, past the old rectory, down the lane. Quiet now but alive during the day with children playing hopscotch, as she did herself in what now seemed like a lifetime ago.

This time as their lips touched the tenderness had turned to urgency. The love that had brought such joy that her heart almost leapt out of her chest, now caused her to ache.

Ache so much that she wanted to cry out.

"We'll talk tomorrow," Matt was aching too. She watched him walk down the garden path so many times before, but this time she'd felt every step as if holding on to a cliff's edge and losing grip!

Chapter Four

"Night Nan," June knew, although in bed hours since Nan would be lying waiting for her familiar footsteps on the stairs.

"Night, night!"

No reply, tonight must be later than she thought.

Even at twenty-six June could expect words in the morning. "Any respectable girl would be in bed by midnight," Nan would huff and puff over breakfast, June would apologise and that would be that, on with the day.

She awoke late next morning, still exhausted. After lying awake for hours, the daylight had brought relief, relief had brought sleep. But not enough, before it was time to get up and face the day.

All was quiet in the kitchen. No Nan letting off steam, no kettle on the boil. For a moment, June didn't think, "Cup of tea would be nice."

Then panic struck, Nan should be up! She hadn't answered goodnight last night!

June didn't remember climbing the stairs, opening the bedroom door, or even picking Nan off the floor!

All she could think of now was to get help, though knowing in her heart it was too late. There was a deathly cold feeling off her wrinkled skin and a stiffness to her now frail body, the room seemed somewhat eerie and June just sat holding her nan in her arms until she'd cried enough.

God she would miss her, not only her jolly presence around the place but the hundreds of things she'd taken for granted in the past. Nan always being there, dinner on the table, kettle on the boil.

Silly things, everyday things that you don't miss until they are no longer there!

Even down to the night before, June hadn't thought anything of Nan not saying goodnight. She'd taken it for granted and fallen asleep, she should have checked.

Maybe she could have done something, maybe she'd be alive today, and at the very least, maybe Nan wouldn't have died alone! Matt was wonderful. She could not have gone through those few days without him, could not have faced the weeks ahead without his support.

Grief had taken its toll, as it does. Sadness had turned to anger, anger in turn had turned to fear, fear to loneliness and then came the reality of it all.

June cried every day, there was such a vacancy in her life now with Nan gone.

'For Sale', the 'Mary Ellen' had brought lots of interest, many offers. She was a lovely boat. Round these parts, there were lots of boats, but only the basic fishing boats, strong and sturdy not much attention to detail.

The 'Mary Ellen' had style, Matt struggled with his decision. Since Nan had passed on he'd been even closer to June, getting on with his life now, following his dreams brought doubts. America was all he'd ever dreamt about.

The 'Mary Ellen' had given him the freedom of taking off into the sunset, pulling into the different harbours, tasting the local traditions. But never had he tasted anything so sweet as to not want to leave it behind!

Would June have changed her mind now Nan wasn't around any longer and didn't depend on her being here there?

Or was there something else that had a hold on her here?

Maybe she didn't love him, maybe... Matt had to stop, his mind was racing. He would give it a little more time. There this was no time for change, there had already been more than enough of that for June. She was heartbroken after her nan and he wasn't going to add to it!

He would wait.

Chapter Five

It was like living through a nightmare these past few months. So many mixed emotions, June didn't remember feeling like this after Pop died. Sure, she had missed him, and still did, but Nan! It was as if her whole world had collapsed that day. She hadn't realised she was such a big part of her life. This was the hardest goodbye.

June had dropped out of school early to help with the chores. There were no regular friends to speak of, at least not many of her own age. She'd spent a lot of time with her pop and his mates, and the rest of her time just being there with her nan. Then Matt came into her life.

Dear Matt! She knew he was holding off, she knew his dreams of America were being put on the back boiler for her now. It was just like him to be so considerate, so selfless.

Nevertheless, it was time now to move on, whatever that meant!

"One day at a time," that was what old Walter had said as he squeezed her hand so tight the day of the burial.

"One day at a time," as he walked away, tears streaming down his weathered face. June loved the old folk around here.

They were of a different era, they had such qualities, and had time to give.

"I know what you need," Matt had caught her daydreaming, again. Just back from 'The Forge,' the blacksmiths in the next village. He'd taken a few hours there doing the books filling in for Millie, who had taken ill.

Matt had crept up behind June tending to Nan's geraniums in the porch. They were her pride and joy, already looking neglected and sad.

"You need a break away from here, there's a fair next week. Let's go! Big city, big shops, we'll take the train stay over for a few days in a posh hotel, what do you think?"

June was tempted, but no it wouldn't be right, not with Nan barely cold in the grave. Then she thought, *Yes, why not!*

Matt had done so much for her, put his plans on hold, even took the few hours at 'The Forge' to pay his way. It was misfortunate Millie had taken ill, but Pop always said,

"'Tis an ill wind that doesn't do someone good."

Yes she would put her own feelings on hold and give Matt some quality time, might do her good too!

As the train pulled out of the station, June felt the thrill of excitement brought her back. They used to pack a picnic in the old days and head off to the fair.

Never stayed at any posh hotels in those days, no!

It would be a day trip. Her nan and pop and half the village. Would be nice to stay at a hotel. She looked at Matt and smiled. If only, things could be left on the back boiler!

But she wasn't going to think about that now, plenty of time for that. She was going to relish every moment of these few days, and she did.

All too soon it was over and Matt was right, it had done her good, she'd felt revitalised, more able to cope, more able to think straight. She'd slept most of the journey home, to be awoken by the whistle of the train letting folk know they were soon to arrive at their destination.

You could see the sea as the train glided in along the tracks.

Matt sitting opposite watched her every move, while she slept and as she awoke.

Their eyes met with a feeling of contentment, June caught a glimpse of the sea in the distance. She'd smiled as if to see an old friend.

"You look happy," Matt took her hand in his.

"Isn't it a wonderful sight—it's like I suffocate when I'm away from it, like I can't breathe."

Without realising it, without even having to ask, June had answered Matt's question.

Chapter Six

Old Walter had been hurt while tying up a rope he slipped between the quay wall and the boat.

There was panic on the quayside, his leg was caught in the weed and he was being dragged under.

Matt, who was just back from 'The Forge' after another uneventful day at the books, noticed the commotion.

Holding on for dear life, Walter looked pale and frightened. Matt didn't hesitate, "Be careful, there's a current." A cry from the crowd was ignored.

Matt could hardly see an inch ahead with the weed and the boat overhead, he struggled, feeling his way to where Walters's leg was tangled in the weed.

A few tugs and it was free, shaken but none the worse for the experience, Walter shook his hand, "You're a good lad."

Didn't look quite the part in Matt's tracksuit but once in dry clothes and sipping his third hot whiskey, Walter had recovered. Matt thought about the 'Mary Ellen'. It was a good offer.

'The Williams Bro's' had a fleet of cruisers down south. They ran day trips for tourists.

He would take her out, get the wind in her sails for the last time.

June had taken a part time job, in the post office.

Didn't pay much but gave her something to do, a reason to get up in the morning. There was only so much you could do around the house, and with Nan at rest now, there was nothing to hold her there all day.

She'd needed something, Matt was wonderful but even he, she thought, needed something other than doing books for Millie at 'The Forge'.

He would lose his spirit, she would talk to him in the evening, let him know she was okay.

She felt he was there sometimes in body only, his heart was somewhere else, following his dreams!

Maybe if he thought she was happy for him to go, he would do what he really wanted to do and find his true happiness.

And she could fall to pieces without shattering someone else's life along with her own! She loved Matt with every inch of her being, she didn't want him to go, but she didn't want him to stay either for the wrong reasons!

Sure, he'd told her he loved her, but as Pop used to say, "You can't keep a butterfly in a jar, maybe it's beautiful to look at, and you may want to hold on to it for yourself but it's going to die!"

That's that, its official, the 'Mary Ellen' was now SOLD!

Matt threw himself on Pop's old chair as if exhausted. "C'mere you," June sat on his lap.

"One of these days this chair will collapse with the weight of the pair of us," she wanted to make light of the moment.

The sale was on the cards for a long time, but now it was final, what was he feeling?

Bound to feel a bit sad, she thought.

"Let's go for a drink to celebrate."

Well if he was sad, he didn't show it! Maybe he was glad, maybe she wouldn't have to talk to him this evening and tell him it was okay for him to pursue his dreams, maybe she was getting cold feet!

Yet again, things would be put on the back boiler! The summer evenings were beginning to have a feel of autumn about them, soon the winter chill would fill the air. Millie was back at 'The Forge' and Matt was happy to hand over the books!

Chapter Seven

"Post for you," June was tending to Nan's geraniums in the back porch, looking much better now they were getting a bit of attention, Matt was waving a letter in his hand from the kitchen. *Dear June*.

"Everything okay?" Matt had cleared off the breakfast table and come back out to the porch to find June in a state of disbelief. "It's from Valerie!"

"Valerie? Who's Valerie?" Matt playfully lifted June in the air.

"No Matt, stop!"

There were tears in her eyes,

"What's the matter?" Matt held her chin up to his as tears streamed down her face. "Valerie's my mom!"

"But…" Matt hadn't realised, there was never any mention of June's mother, only that she'd taken a hike and left her for her grandparents to rear all those years ago.

That was the only time June had spoken about her mother, why was she writing to her now?

"She's in town next week, wants to meet," June wiped away the tears.

"Why after all these years, not a postcard or a phone call to see how you were, why now?" Matt couldn't make sense of it.

"I don't know, what should I do Matt? I don't remember her, I have no feelings for her."

"*Ssh*," Matt held her close. She felt small and fragile like a frightened little bird that had fallen from a tree.

June passed the café on the corner, must be ten times.

She could see someone sitting, but with their back to the window she couldn't see the face. Even if she had been looking her in the face, she couldn't be sure she would recognise her anyway.

Sure she'd heard bits and pieces in the past but nothing much. Valerie wasn't exactly flavour of the month with Nan!

She'd come this far (against Matt's advice and her own better judgement), she would go two steps further and deal with this.

"C'mon June, can't be that bad," she'd told herself.

As she walked towards her, June could see the resemblance.

Only half her age, but you could be looking at Nan!

A middle-aged woman who looked just as June felt, scared and apprehensive. She stood up as June came closer, for what seemed like an eternity they both stood in silence.

"Ready to order?" the waiter oblivious to the situation, ready to pounce with his pen and jotter.

"Tea for me," June said.

"Tea for two," Valerie added, "Please, sit. I wasn't sure if you'd come, this place hasn't changed much," Valerie looked out of the window, across towards the quayside where time seemed to stand still. Just up the road a bit, and across the bridge you had new developments all right, lots of hustle and bustle.

But by the quay side was always the same, June liked its serenity, its peace.

"Why now," June felt nothing, no remorse no resentment, nothing!

Valerie was as a stranger to her, how could she feel anything.

"Don't let her upset you," Matt had given her a good luck kiss, although he'd have preferred she had ignored the letter altogether!

"June, I am so sorry, so very sorry."

Then there was a silence, so loud you could almost hear it. "Let's get out of here, go for a walk."

The café, though practically empty at this time was getting claustrophobic!

They walked without a word, down onto the beach, the air so fresh now, cool but wonderful.

Nature had a way of putting things into perspective!

"Nan and Pop have passed on."

"I know," Valerie interrupted, "met old Walter this morning, had a stroll down around earlier, showed me where they were buried. You're not the first I've apologised to today, didn't think Walter would recognise me. Brought some geraniums, she used to love them."

June felt numb.

"June. I know this is hard for you to understand, but I was sixteen! Scared, ignorant, curious. I don't know what you'd call it, STUPID, I suppose and naive!"

There was a gentle ripple at the water's edge, "Was he from 'round here?" June didn't really care, didn't know why she even asked, it just sort of came out.

"Roger was a married man, said it was a marriage of convenience. His wife's family owned the business where he worked."

"We loved each other June, we really did."

"We were together even after you were born for a while, not living together, obviously! I was in enough trouble! Had brought enough shame! We used to meet on the quiet, made plans to go off, all three of us. You, Roger or 'Red' as they called him because of his red hair, and me. Wasn't aware he was planning to pay our way by stealing the takings from where he worked."

"He wasn't aware they were on to him either! Was sacked on the spot, his name all over the papers, couldn't take the shame. After days of being missing, he was found in an old barn, he had hung himself. I was so angry, angry with him, angry with the world, angry with God. But mostly angry at the local paper, they'd had a field day."

"Got wind of his fancy piece having a baby then to add to his shame. I'm not saying what he did wasn't wrong, it was. But they hounded him, drove him to it! It was awful."

"I'm not exactly proud of what I did either but I was out of my mind June. I went to their printing office and I sprayed paint all over their window and door, destroyed it."

"Next day we had the guards at the door! Hadn't noticed the security camera in front of the building!"

"Caught red-handed! Your nan went on about it for weeks. Under the circumstances, with me having a small baby and all, I got off with a caution. In my mind, there was only one thing to do. Get as far away from here as I could."

"I loved you June, but I wasn't in any position to bring up a child. I had a live-in cleaning job."

Valerie's thoughts seemed to wander, "Can still smell your hair, still remember the softness of your skin! Well the rest is history!"

"Did you know his wife?" June wanted to know more.

"She left town, don't know much more about her."

"But," June started, "all those years, why now?" she was curious, "How could you say you loved someone, yet leave and not get in touch for, how many years?"

Didn't make sense to her!

Seems Valerie had kept in touch! Christmas, birthdays! All returned to her unopened by Nan!

"She must have really hated me, can't say I blame her, the only consolation was, I knew she was still there for you when they were returned."

"When you became twenty-one, I sent my last card, sad but it was the only way I had of keeping in touch. As time went on, it got harder and harder to go back, then you leave it too late eh? No good wishing at this stage."

Chapter Eight

June didn't know whether to feel sorry for her or to hate her. She'd seen hate in Nan's eyes, with the mention of Valerie's name. Pop would mention her sometimes.

It eats you up inside. In a similar situation, what would she have done, she wondered.

Who knows? Maybe the same, maybe not!

It's all very well in hindsight. Circumstances can change a person! Valerie got up to go, she had hoped for some sort of bond, maybe even reconciliation between them.

But there was nothing, she was as a stranger to her daughter, she had left it till too late! She was paying dearly for her mistakes. Maybe their paths would cross again, maybe one day, June might come looking for her.

June sat and watched some canoeists struggle against the current to go upstream, their vibrant colours reflecting on the water. *Sometimes*, she thought, *life could be like that, an uphill struggle!*

She suddenly felt alone, Nan and Pop gone and now Matt, well, she had Matt but how long before he would want to pursue his dreams!

America had still come up in conversation, but he hadn't pushed her.

She knew he was biding his time and then she would really be alone.

Why hadn't she even tried to understand Valerie, why had she not felt any closeness with her, she had given her birth for God's sake! Had Nan instilled in her the hate she'd felt for Valerie herself? So much so, that it had blocked out any feelings at all she might have had? June watched as Valerie walked over the little footbridge, over the quays and on until she was out of sight.

If she'd felt nothing, why was she feeling this loneliness?

She opened the piece of paper Valerie had put in her hand as she walked away. It would have been so easy to dial that number, maybe someday, maybe tomorrow, maybe never!

"Penny for your thoughts?" Matt leaned over June's shoulder and held her.

"Oh Matt!" It was like a dam had burst and all her emotions had come flooding out, she sobbed uncontrollably.

"What am I like?" They sat without saying a word, Matt had a way of making things all right, soothing the hurt, and she wanted to sit there forever.

Matt spent days preparing the 'Mary Ellen' for her last trip out of the harbour. He would hand her over to her new owner at the end of the week. He'd pleaded with June to accompany him.

Weather permitting the journey would take about three days.

They could hire a car and take in some scenery on the way back. "Not a chance, a trip around the bay was one thing but three days at sea! It'll be like a death sentence." June never did find her sea legs. Pop had often said he'd never seen so many colours in a girl's face at one time, after he'd taken her out on the bay.

"I'll miss you," as Walter threw the ropes to him, Matt whispered from the deck.

"Me too," June stood as the distance between grew further and further, "more than you'll ever know."

"A brave man," Walter tipped his cap to wish him fair winds.

"He'll be fine," June reassured her old friend.

"Aw, the sea, can be friend or foe," Walter went on his way as June watched until the 'Mary Ellen' was but a spec on the horizon.

"Godspeed."

The days now shorter as the autumn winds chilled the air, and the nights seemed so long without Matt. It had been four days, surely there would be word soon. If anything had happened, she would have heard, wouldn't she?

"No news is good news," Pop used to say.

Chapter Nine

June loved the autumn colours in the garden. Reminded her of the cosy nights snuggled up in Pop's old chair by the fire.

Nice memories! Would she ever feel that contentment again, that feeling of being loved and secure? So long ago now, it seemed like another lifetime. A character in a book she'd read perhaps!

"Any word from the traveller?" Walter stood at the counter, it was pension day at the post office. She enjoyed her few hours working there, but these days her mind was elsewhere.

"Sorry Walter, was miles away. No, no word from Matt," there was concern in her voice. "And how are you Walter?"

"Aw sure, pulling the devil by the tail, a girl, pulling the devil by the tail."

"Dear Walter, now don't you be fretting, he'll be fine." And putting his pension book safely inside his, now well-worn top coat he tipped his hat and was on his way.

As she walked up the garden path, June could hear the phone ringing in the hall. All fingers and thumbs she finally managed to get the key in the door.

"Hi Ju," Matt had run into some problems on the way and had just docked. He would have all the paperwork sorted by the weekend and be on his way back. Her heart wanted to say, "Hurry back, I'm lost without you."

Her head, if she had listened, would say, "Keep going Matt, now we've made the break, it would be so much easier than having to say goodbye again." The latter being inevitable.

It was the weekend. And although she loved her few hours in the post office, June looked forward to the weekend.

No rush to get out of bed, no hurry to get out of your pyjamas! The autumn was settling in nicely, boats all tied up, even on the worst of days the village looked pretty.

June had asked herself over and over again over the last couple of weeks. What if, what if Matt were to go to America? Would she be okay with that? Would she maybe go with him should he ask her again? Would he ask her again?

She had missed him, her days were empty without him.

But was America for her?

Matt, as if on the same line of thought, had decided he was going to ask June again about America. He hoped her answer this time would be yes!

He'd hoped she'd missed him as much as he'd missed her while he'd been away.

"Here to collect a special parcel," June looked up from her files, filing was the one part of the job that she hated, but someone had to do it and Clodagh wasn't a fan either!

"Matt," Clodagh looking on smiling, "Go on you two lovebirds, I'll finish up here." There would be no argument from June! She was out of there with a smile on her face.

Clodagh was such an easy person to work for, never married, a waste, June thought, she had a nice motherly way about her, would have made a lovely mom, kind and caring.

Never lost for words they chatted and cuddled all the way home, and once there, they chatted and cuddled some more!

"Missed you," Matt's touch on her skin made her tingle, just lying in each other's arms it felt…so right.

"Wait," Matt took across the room at an awful rate, "I have a present for you."

June smiled, sometimes he could be like a big child.

"It's not much," he handed her an object wrapped in an oily cloth.

"What is it?" June unwrapped what looked like a piece of steel.

"Turn it over," Matt reached for the steel plate and turned it over to the other side that revealed the name 'The Mary Ellen'.

"But," June looked at Matt.

"The new owners have renamed her as part of their fleet so they asked if I wanted it as a keepsake," Matt's eyes so full of sincerity.

"I want you to have it Ju, it's what brought us together."

Chapter Ten

The weeks passed, and winter stole in so quickly behind the autumn, that it almost went unnoticed.

Weather bound, with their fishing boats all tied up the locals were grounded. Walter was waving a letter in his hand as he came running up the garden path,

"June! June! It's Lily! She's…she's," June meeting him half way.

"Walter slow down, catch your breath."

"Come quickly! I think something is up with Lily, she's just…" June followed Walter as he took off down the road.

They only lived a few minutes away, she'd spent many an afternoon helping Lily after school.

They'd had hens and June would collect the eggs for her, often bringing home a basket full for tea.

They were lovely people, got married late in life, Nan used to say and never had children.

Lily had passed away peacefully in her chair, June called the emergency services, then Matt.

She did all she could to help poor Walter. He looked so frail and lost and old! Matt was a great help and once word went round the village there was a path worn to the door, home-made cakes, scones apple tarts, brown bread.

People were so thoughtful and genuinely caring.

Walters's heart was breaking, but there would be no outward show, he would carry his wounds and soldier on.

Still holding the letter he looked up at June, "Picked it up off the floor, was bringing it in for Lily to read, never can find the glasses when you need them."

Poor Walter.

As the rain lashed against the window, there was a long silence.

Holding her hand, still warm he gasped.

"Shh," June hoped her presence had been of some comfort to him. The ceremony was plain and simple. Exhausted after a couple of very long days, Walter left the graveyard and the love of his life in the cold earth. June sat with him once everyone had gone, he'd chatted about old times, he laughed and he cried! The kitchen walls laced with old photographs, so many memories.

On the sideboard were Walters's old trophies of his hurling days, polished proudly every Saturday religiously by Lily.

She'd watched her often as a child.

"He's a good lad, Matt, has a heart of gold," Walter's hand was cold as June took it to reassure him,

"I'll always be here for you, you know that don't you?"

She knew Matt was slowly but surely winning her heart too and it scared her!

"We'll not get another year out of this lot," June held the chair as Clodagh struggled with the tinsel, it did make the small post office look pretty.

Didn't really feel like Christmas, June thought, *wind and rain but no sign of snow!* Christmas without Nan was a very lonely time and she wasn't looking forward to it.

She remembered the first Christmas without Pop, it had been a lonely one, but Nan being Nan had made the most of it.

Turkey, ham, and all the trimmings! Even lit the pudding, as was tradition! June wondered how she'd had the heart to do it.

"Won't feel it now," Clodagh was getting into the spirit of things. June envied her sometimes, always seemed content, taking each day as it came.

"Life could give you happiness...but could also take it away without any warning... It's up to you to make the most of the time in between," she used to say.

Chapter Eleven

She would make an effort and enjoy the season.

Maybe ask Walter around for the Christmas dinner. Ya, that would be nice.

As Clodagh reached to put up the last bit of tinsel, June could feel the chair go with her, and bringing tinsel and all with her she fell to the floor!

"Damn," they both laughed, there was nothing else they could do! It was after all the season to be jolly!

"Something smells nice," Matt came into the kitchen looking sleepy. June had been up since early morning to get started on dinner, she tried to remember all that Nan had taught her but still fretted!

"What if it's not properly cooked? What if everyone's sick with food poisoning after eating?"

All flushed and bothered, she greeted Matt with a smile.

"Merry Christmas," Matt giggled as he wiped a bit of stuffing from her nose.

"Merry Christmas."

Walter snored the afternoon away, stuffed with turkey and ham and all the trimmings, a couple of bottles of Guinness and he was away.

June sat at Matt's feet looking into the blazing fire.

"This is nice," as she looked up at Matt, he pointed to the window. The light now fading, it had begun to snow. With contentment in his voice, Matt leaned forward and kissed the top of her head.

"Merry Christmas."

Walter was missing Lily, it was still very early days and still very raw, very raw indeed. His eyes filled with tears at the mention of her name. June kept an eye on him, brought some dinner over from time to time (in passing).

Walter wouldn't hear of anyone going out of their way for him, and on the rare occasion when she did bake she always remembered him.

"I'll not forget yer kindness," Walter was always so appreciative of the smallest thought. "Was thinking I might get some of Lily's things together for the charity shop, no sense leaving them there to rot. Someone might make use of them."

"That would be a lovely thing to do," June felt for him, it had to be a hard thing to do.

"Want me to come and give you a hand?" There were bags of clothes, Lily loved to dress, some still with their tags on. All bagged and ready for collection in the hall they sat down to have a cup of tea.

Looking 'round the kitchen, Walter looked thoughtful, "There's some things I could never part with," he was finding this harder than he thought. As he poured the tea, he handed June a little red velvet bag, drawn together with a gold string. "It was Lily's, she'd want you to have it."

As June opened the little bag, she felt so touched she couldn't hold back the tears, it had taken all her might to be strong for Walter, all day watching him go through Lily's stuff with a broken heart. It was all too much she couldn't hold back the tears any longer, some help she turned out to be, blubbering all over the place.

"Oh! Walter…it's lovely…I couldn't."

"Sure 'tisn't much, I want you to have it, so would Lily," as he pinned the brooch to June's cardigan.

"All these years, she kept it all these years, it was the first present I ever bought her. Saved for weeks, always said it was the best present she ever got. Must be near on forty years ago now,"

"I shall treasure it, Walter, thank you," she hugged the old man and left him with his memories. Life could be so sad!

Chapter Twelve

Walking home, June thought about Matt, he seemed happy, but what had become of his plans?

Of course, she wanted him to stay but she hoped he wasn't holding off to suit her, she would talk to him tonight.

As she turned the key in the door, she could smell food, he hadn't mentioned bringing home a take-away for tea!

With candles on the table Matt greeted her, tea towel on his arm, he guided her to her chair, "Like to taste the wine, madam?"

"What's the occasion?" June was baffled it wasn't her birthday, that was next month.

"Today, my dear June, is the anniversary of the day our eyes met across a counter of eggs. Happy pancake Tuesday," they both laughed.

She hadn't really thought.

Matt could be so romantic, not a bad cook either, could give her a run for her money anytime.

He poured them a second glass of wine, "A toast!" he raised his glass, "To the future and new beginnings," as their glasses clashed June felt her heart sink.

Matt took her hand in his and kissed it, with hope in his heart, "Come with me to see the world."

Matt had often heard it said, the eyes never lie, they are the windows to the soul. There was no need for words he knew what the answer was. June couldn't talk, how could she tell him that each day she had hoped that things would go on as they were, and that someday, Matt would forget about America and seeing the world and maybe see his world in her.

They cleared the table and washed up in silence, this was Junes favourite time of the day, they would argue about who would wash and who would dry and talk about the events of the day, not very exciting to some but she loved to hear about Matt's day and he hers. It was like filling in the gaps of the time that they had been apart.

June hadn't had her mind on her work for days but today it seemed neither did Clodagh.

"You okay?" she thought how they had become more like old friends in the past year than employer and employee. Clodagh looked back at June.

"Ya, I'm fine," she couldn't lie to save her life.

June didn't push her, she would talk when she was ready. Clodagh, as if knowing what she was thinking smiled at her friend, "Want to go for a drink later?" June knew her friend needed to talk but at the counter of a busy post office on a Friday (pension day) was hardly ideal.

"Ya, okay."

As she hurriedly had her shower and got ready to meet Clodagh, Matt came in. Still a bit distant since their conversation a couple of days before.

"Going out," almost avoiding eye contact but not quite, Matt looked at her admiringly.

"Meeting Clodagh for a drink," normally she would have asked Matt to join them and Clodagh wouldn't have minded but tonight she wanted to give Clodagh a chance to talk if she wanted to and if Matt was there she wouldn't do that.

Even so, she still might not but at least she would give her the opportunity.

"June, I'm sorry. I've been a prat," June didn't need much encouragement to fall into Matt's arms.

"Let's forget about it," and when Matt took her in his arms she melted all over again.

As she watched her friend approach, she thought to herself, Clodagh never seemed the least bit interested in attracting the opposite sex but always took great interest in her appearance. Although where she got the time, June often wondered, with running the post office which she'd taken over from an aunt of hers years since.

Some say she could have been anything she'd wanted, brains to burn but she choose not to go any further with her education. Coming from a family of academics, seems her folks were somewhat disappointed that she didn't pursue a 'proper career'.

Chapter Thirteen

Her dad was a dentist and her mother a teacher, Nan used to say they'd had great hopes for their only daughter, but Clodagh had other ideas. She'd spent all of her summer holidays as a child helping in the post office and every Saturday during the school year.

Doreen, Clodagh's aunt had returned from America, having worked all the hours God sent over there, had gone off in her teens to find work and make her fortune.

Some say she had helped to put Clodagh's dad through college.

She'd invested in the post office, never married.

After her sudden death at the age of sixty-two, it seems relations came from everywhere for the reading of her will. It was to their great disappointment that she had left a great deal of her estate to her favourite charity and the post office to Clodagh.

Being in her final year in school before going on to college, as Clodagh's parents hoped she would do, Clodagh had a very big decision to make.

The post office would be closed until further notice, of course it would be different running the place herself but Clodagh's mind was made up, as soon as she was of age she would take up the running of the post office as was her inheritance and her aunt Doreen's wish. She would be set up for life.

Clodagh enrolled for a course for two years doing accountancy, which would bring her up to her eighteenth birthday and the beginning of the rest of her life, though going against her parent's wishes, she felt it was the right choice for her.

It would be hard work and long hours but she was determined to make a go of it and in time her parents would accept her decision, after all it was her life!

She had indeed given it everything, to the extent that she had no life outside of the business, but she was happy.

Her parents now retired had accepted their disappointment but often reminded her that she could have done better in life.

In their day, it was a struggle to get a proper education, in their opinion Clodagh was being handed the opportunity on a plate.

It didn't make sense to them that she wouldn't take advantage of it.

The post office could be sold and she could have had a nice nest egg.

Aunt Doreen was so different from her dad, Clodagh would tell her they were like chalk and cheese. Educated by life experiences, Doreen always said, "Life is the best educator. Life teaches you more than any text book ever could. Takes more than academics to run the world, just be happy dear, whatever you decide to do, that's what's important. There's room for everyone."

Clodagh would listen to Doreen go on and on, sometimes not making any sense to her back then but as she grew older and even now, she'd often think back and a lot of it made sense. "If life teaches you one thing, Clodagh dear, it's not to waste a moment of your time and especially not to waste it living out someone else's dreams," she used to say, "You make your own happiness."

She smiled as she saw her enter struggling with her umbrella and the narrow café door.

"You waiting long?" catching her breath, she apologised for being late.

After their third cup of coffee and as much small talk as June could take, she was no longer going to avoid the issue. Clodagh had something on her mind and June felt she was bursting to talk about it.

"You okay?" June would make the first move.

"Ya, no. Oh! I don't know June, I guess I've come to a crossroads in my life."

Chapter Fourteen

June listened as her friend went on.

"I know I am better off than most and I haven't one regret in life but," there were tears in her eyes as Clodagh continued, "It's just well."

"Another cuppa," June called the waiter.

"June, telling you this is probably the only part I am struggling with, my mind is quite clear about everything else but my decision also affects you unfortunately. I have decided to sell up. Not immediately of course, it'll be six months or more. Enough time for you to get yourself another job."

"Hey, don't be worrying about me. I'm a survivor remember I'll be grand," they both laughed.

June hadn't noticed Clodagh being unsettled or anything of the sort, quite the contrary in fact she'd often envied her, her status in life.

Not a care in the world, no money worries although Nan always said money wasn't everything and if she knew June had envied her friend or any other person for that matter she would turn in her grave, envy was a sin and we should be happy with our lot, that's what Nan used to say.

"You're not ill?" June was worried for a moment.

"No, nothing like that. It's difficult to explain," Clodagh went on, "As you know, I work round the clock and I'm not complaining, don't get me wrong. It's just, well who am I doing it for? No children to leave all my millions to," they had a giggle, "I want to do something with my time. Make a difference, ya know?"

"So what will you do?" June couldn't make out where this was all going.

"I'm going to volunteer for charity work in Africa. June my assets would be invaluable out there, maybe build an orphanage or a school, at the very least I can be on hand to help out. If it doesn't work out, I can always come back. At least, I'd have done something."

June didn't know what to say,

"Sort of an aid worker is it."

"Yes. June I have given it a lot of thought."

June wanted to support her friend, though it meant her looking for a new job but that wasn't relevant.

"I wish you all the luck in the world," she hugged Clodagh, "I will miss you though," Clodagh smiled, a smile that had relief written all over it.

"I'm so glad I have told you now. Thought you'd tell me I was cracked. Thanks June for not judging me, I know many will but this is something I want to do while I am still able. If I should only help one person out there, it will have been worth it, I will have made a difference."

Matt was surprised to hear about Clodagh's plans

"Strange. Wouldn't have thought she was the type to go half way across the world."

June felt a bit sad at the thought of losing such a good friend, and her job as well of course, but mostly not having Clodagh around. They had become good friends and even though she truly wished her well, June knew she would miss her terribly.

"Suppose it's something she wants to do, seems like she's been thinking about it for some time now."

Matt handed June the last of the plates to dry, "All done. You'll miss her now won't you? Never know sure maybe someone might take over the post office and at least you'd still have your job."

Chapter Fifteen

"Maybe, we'll see," if June had any previous doubts about Matt's future plans she certainly hadn't any now, not after their little anniversary celebration the other night. She knew now it was about time to 'set the butterfly free'.

"Matt. We need to talk," June loved that stupid grin Matt would wear as if he didn't know what was coming next.

"Sounds serious," she laughed and took him by the hand and sat him down in Pop's old armchair.

"It is serious."

Matt's expression changed.

"Just let me say what I have to say. It's taken me so long to do this. Please Matt. Don't make it any harder."

Matt listened intently not knowing what he was going to hear. Was there something wrong? Had he done something to upset her?

"I want you to follow your dream, go to America, see the world! I love you Matt. I can't be happy watching you living a lie. Do it for me."

There was a long silence, Matt said nothing, this wasn't the reaction June had expected, she didn't know what exactly she did expect but certainly not this—no reaction at all. She could think of nothing to say now, so much to be said and she could think of absolutely nothing to say.

In all of their time together, she had never once felt awkward in his presence, not until now.

For what seemed like an eternity, but could only have been minutes Matt just sat and stared at the floor, then he got up and walked towards the door.

He said nothing as he turned round to look at June, tears streaming down his face and proceeded to go out of the door. "Matt…"

Not closing it angrily, just gently as was his way and he had gone.

"Matt…"

June curled up on Pop's old armchair and cried her fill.

It was a week later, June went round to Walter's with some shepherd's pie, he loved shepherd's pie, least he'd loved Lily's shepherd's pie. June wasn't sure hers was up to Lily's standard but he'd never complained.

"Penny for them," Walter had been standing holding a plate of custard creams.

"I'm sorry Walter, I was miles away," June burst into tears, "Matt's gone. He's gone Walter."

With a gentle hand on her shoulder, it was Walter's turn to comfort her.

"There, there, he'll not have gone far with a heavy heart. There, there."

Chapter Sixteen

Matt was overdue a visit home, the bus journey seemed to take forever, he shouldn't have walked out like that but why would June tell him she loved him and in the same breath tell him to go, to go thousands of miles away to follow his dream, a dream that was now becoming a nightmare.

He had kept in touch with his mother all the time but never felt the desire to return home, until now.

Awoken by the movement on the bus Matt was somewhat relieved to finally be there. Mind you, it wasn't a 'good to be home' feeling just relieved at the journey's end.

He had come from a strange background, his mother a heart of gold had spent every waking hour catering to the demands of his alcoholic father. There were no great bonds with his father, he would spend his time adapting to his father's moods to keep the peace while his mother would cover up the bruises!

Matt had promised himself that once he was old enough to make his own way he would work hard to make a life for himself far away from there.

His mother, put down so often began to believe she was worthless, self-esteem crushed to the core, why anyone would take such abuse and cover it up, Matt couldn't understand.

He'd pleaded and pleaded with her time and time again to leave him but she 'loved him' and he 'loved her' and never meant to hurt her, it was the drink you see, she would say to Matt, some way of showing it he'd thought, this was mental abuse and nothing less!

Nothing had changed, his mother overjoyed to see him still bore the bruises of a recent mood swing, it was so hard to turn a blind eye to what was going on. It had driven Matt away.

"Please Matt, he doesn't mean it."

Same old words, he would have to respect his mother's wishes. He was powerless.

Clodagh was busy these last couple of weeks, she'd made contact with the volunteer group and was all but ready to take off. The business side of things however were slower to organise. The post office was up for sale to be taken on, she hoped as a going concern, that way June might still have a job and her local pensioners, of which there weren't so many these days only the few, wouldn't have to travel to the city to collect their pension. But Clodagh had given them a good service all those years and not one could wish her anything but the best of luck.

"Indeed, you'll be missed around here," Mrs Mac as everyone knew her, Mrs McCarty being her proper name, bundled her few messages into her shopping bag and collected her change from the counter.

"Indeed, in you will a girl," and she walked towards the door leaving her shopping bag down for a moment to fix her scarf and open the door.

"Take care Mrs Mac," Clodagh would miss this too.

The only way of life she'd known for so many years now.

The fresh eggs that Greta down the road would bring knowing that in return Clodagh would bring her the best brown soda bread anyone ever baked.

And there was Nancy in the village who'd pick her first daffodils and bring them to the post office to put in the window, simple thoughtful folk, the likes of whom Clodagh knew she would probably never meet again. She would indeed miss them.

June hadn't noticed the clock tick so loudly before, it was five thirty in the morning and she longed for daylight to come. Twisting and turning all night long these days she was more exhausted in the mornings than rested, she had come to hate the darkness.

Was it time to give up on Matt! It had been three weeks now and no word.

What about his things? He'd taken nothing with him only what he was wearing, he always travelled light anyway, she'd thought to herself, there wasn't much stuff to leave behind.

Chapter Seventeen

She wondered what he was doing now, right at this moment. Was he lying awake maybe wondering about her?

Maybe he'd moved on, maybe. June tormented with thoughts and maybe's decided to get up and face the day.

If only, she could switch off for a while, if only she knew he was okay. Perhaps today, perhaps he'd ring today!

Weeks turned into months and June had long since reconciled herself that Matt had moved on, had gone for good.

As she walked down, through the village towards the post office, she gasped as the 'SOLD' sign went up on the post office. Although, knowing it was about to happen at any time, June was still set aback to actually see it.

Clodagh was grinning from ear to ear as June entered the post office.

"Great news! The sale went through yesterday afternoon."

"I'm so happy for you," June hugged her friend and was genuinely happy for her. As far as she herself was concerned, her future was unsure but she would support her friend all the way.

She'd only wished she herself had the courage to go further afield, but something was holding her here, she would never ask to leave though what held her here was a complete mystery to her.

The quayside was dotted with lunchtime sun worshipers, summer had taken everyone by surprise and arrived early.

There were solicitors, barristers, shop assistants, doctors, people from every walk of life, June thought to herself as she walked along towards the quayside herself with her take away coffee hoping to find a quiet corner to take in a few of the sun's rays.

She jerked as she was touched on the shoulder and turned around.

"How are you?" June was speechless for a moment

"Matt," for a moment there was a feeling of awkwardness, but only for a moment.

Matt didn't stand for much longer, "Enjoying the weather?"

He never was one for small talk.

"June, the way I left, I—"

"All in the past," June wasn't going to tell him she'd thought of that dreadful day on every waking moment.

"I went home, just got back."

Matt had told June about the situation at home when they'd first met.

He'd swore he'd never go back there, he'd rang home every week without fail, he was good to his mother, would send her a few pounds when he had it to spare. But he'd swore he'd never go back there, couldn't bear to watch.

"Is it okay if I come and pick up my stuff sometime? I know it's not much. That is, if you haven't dumped it."

"'Course I haven't. It's no problem pick it up anytime you want."

As he walked away, he turned as he always used to do and waved. June wanted to scream, in jerking to see who was tapping her on the shoulder she'd spilled her (still black, as she hadn't yet put the milk in) coffee and scalded her hand.

She'd held it behind her back while talking to Matt not feeling any pain up until now.

Stupid girl, she thought to herself.

"What did I say," Walter greeted June at the door. June was puzzled.

"He'd not go far. Didn't I say he'd not go far? I was talking to your Matt this afternoon."

June smiled, poor Walter, "Yes. I spoke to him earlier, he's come to pick up his stuff."

"Fiddlesticks. Sure isn't it written all over the lads face."

Chapter Eighteen

"Now Walter, eat up your shepherd's pie and don't be going on with your nonsense," they both laughed.

"Thanks June, I'm very grateful for your trouble, you're a good girl."

June noticed Walter was slowing down a bit, though an active man he was getting on too, she thought, although she'd never known how old he was he'd been collecting his pension now for a while.

"Sure, 'twas no bother at all. Wasn't I doing a bit for myself anyway, have to keep our strength up eh!"

As she walked home with her tea towel in her hand, June thought about her nan, she always said one shouldn't boast about doing good.

"Keep it to yourself," she used to say, "God sees all."

She still missed her nan and pop too. Things were different then, simple. Why must life be so complicated!

These days she was feeling tired, drained. Life could do that sometimes, knock the stuffing out of you.

As she approached the garden gate, June could see Matt standing at her front door. *Tall, slim, a catch for any woman*, she thought, she remembered the first time he'd spoken to her in the local shop.

Funny, she couldn't recall much of her life before meeting Matt, nothing exciting anyway.

He'd been the best thing that had ever happened to her, it was only a pity it had to end like this—a pity it had to end at all.

"Hi," he'd spotted her as she reached over to open the gate, "Is it a good time to call?"

"Ya, 'course," she greeted him with a smile.

No point dragging up the events of the past, she thought, he was only picking up his stuff and he'd be on his way again.

As June closed the door behind them, she offered Matt a cup of tea, she didn't know who owed who an apology, Matt had hurt her in going without a word but perhaps she had hurt him too, she must have or he wouldn't have gone off like that.

"There's shepherd's pie in the oven if you're hungry. Just been down to Walter with some."

Matt sat in Pop's old chair, for a moment it was as if nothing had happened.

"Saw him earlier, seems in good form," Matt suddenly got to his feet, "Maybe I should go. I'll just get my things."

As he went up the stairs of the old cottage, June listened to his footsteps and the old familiar creeks in the floorboards which she hadn't heard for a while being alone in the house, it was nice.

She'd never imagined herself being alone, there was always Nan and Pop and when Pop had passed away, there was Nan and then there was Matt. It didn't really bother her being alone in the house she just never imagined she would be.

In years gone by, she would have given anything to come home and have her own space sometimes, do her own thing.

Pop would have his buddies in for a card game or a few drinks and a singsong.

Now, she'd give anything to have it all back again, a bit of noise about the place.

She heard Matt come down the stairs.

"Kettle's boiled. Have a cuppa before you go."

"June, I am really sorry for the way I left that day, truly. I will always regret it. It was rude, you didn't deserve to be treated like that. I just."

"We all have our regrets," June handed him his tea and his favourite biscuits.

"You doing okay?" he asked sincerely.

"Oh, you know me," they smiled and the conversation became a bit easier, a bit less awkward.

He'd spent the last couple of months at home things were as bad as ever, his dad still drinking the house falling down around them.

Chapter Nineteen

Kept himself busy doing the long overdue repairs, taking all his might not to get involved with their sad life.

Malcolm Mac Phearson came from a business background, his family had shops all over the country. He'd been commuting from one to another of them working under the supervision of his mother and now he wanted to branch out on his own.

The post office was an ideal investment, he'd thought, a well-established business up and running.

Clodagh would take time before she left to show him the ropes, so to speak!

"June, this is Malcom Mac Phearson," Clodagh greeted June as she went through the door of the post office, still thinking about Matt.

They'd chatted for a while the evening before over a cup of tea, she knew she still had feelings for him she just hoped it wasn't evident in their conversation, things were complicated enough. She had to let him get on with his life and get on with her own. June smiled conservatively as she shook the stranger's outstretched hand.

"Pleased to meet you Mr Mac Phearson," he had a firm hold, an assertive look about him, June thought.

"Mac, my friends call me Mac." Was he to be her new boss or had he other plans for the post office, she'd have to wait and see.

He couldn't be more than her own age, maybe a couple of years younger, she thought, but so much worldlier, nice and easy on the eyes too!

"What do you think?" Clodagh had left Malcolm Mac Phearson in the back room going over the books.

"Seems okay," June wondered had he mentioned keeping her on. As if reading her mind, Clodagh reassured her that her job was safe, he would be running the post office as it was and in time hoped to maybe expand into stocking different products.

There was after all an opening for a bigger variety of stock in the grocery end of things. Clodagh only ever carried the necessary bits that would maybe tie someone over until they got to the bigger shops, it was more a convenience store with a post office. She'd never had any big plans, was happy to potter along and make enough to pay the bills and put a bit aside. The sale would bring a nice tidy sum, enough to carry out her plans.

June was relieved to hear that she would still have a job at least, as regards the future she would take it one day at a time.

The doorbell rang, June just out of the shower, hair still dripping opened the door in her dressing gown, "Hi Matt," she hadn't been expecting him today. She was meeting Clodagh for lunch, their last meeting as she was on her way very early in the morning.

Handing the house key to June, Matt smiled.

"Meant to leave it with you the other day."

"Come in, I'm just out of the shower," June stepped aside as Matt walked past her into the hall.

"I'm staying at Walter's for a bit. He offered me his spare room until I get sorted. Better keep going, said I'd do a few jobs for him. Pay for my keep," Matt smiled and they shared a giggle, looking into June's eyes her hair still wet he recalled the happier times.

For a moment, he stared at her beauty, he'd often wondered before how she had managed to stay single. Must have been out of choice, certainly wasn't for the want of offers, he thought.

She had a natural beauty, a glow about her, no beauty products could produce such a result.

"See you then," June was beginning to shiver as she held the door open, Matt standing motionless looking at her.

"Yes, yes thanks June," and he walked down the garden path to the gate. He turned and waved.

Clodagh looked her best, happy and excited about her new adventure.

Chapter Twenty

"Won't be long now," June greeted her friend and they embraced.

"Don't know if I'm more terrified or excited. A bit of both I suppose."

"You'll be grand," June was full of admiration for Clodagh, it took a lot of guts to do what she did, she hoped she would be okay and that everything would work out for her as planned.

"I'm so glad you're staying on at the post office. I think Mac will appreciate it too, he's going to need your support."

June wasn't sure it would be the same working with Mac, but she would give it a go, for the moment it suited her anyway, employment wasn't that easy to come by unless you went into the city and she didn't want to do that.

Mac seemed okay, what little she knew of him at least, he was an ordinary sort of a man, no airs and graces about him.

She didn't know why but June did feel a bit shy in his presence, maybe it was that she'd never worked with a man before, but every time he'd approached her desk to ask her a question or even if he only stood by her or glanced from the other side of the room, she could feel her face go a bright shade of red.

She'd hoped he didn't notice.

Walking along the beach there was a tent. *A two-man tent* June thought, *probably a couple sleeping on after a late night huddled together by the campfire of which there were still the remains of.* It had been a beautiful moonlit night.

The sea softly rippled as if sneaking in so that it wouldn't be noticed.

What was it that kept her here, it wasn't as if she had family now with Nan and Pop having passed on, and they were the only family she'd known apart from her brief encounter with Valerie. Valerie, it had been months now and not a word since.

Although, she had left it up to her to make contact if she'd wanted to, June thought, and where did she leave that piece of paper with Valerie's number on, as if she'd ever ring.

No it was something else, some sort of bond with the place that kept her here, she belonged here especially right here by the rippling sea she'd breath more easily, winter or summer it didn't matter what the weather it was life giving, mind cleansing it held her there.

A stranger passed by and smiled, June now watching the locals gather to meet the fishing boats come in. It was far cheaper to buy the fish directly from the boats, fresher too.

"The shops would have three prices on it," Walter used to say. She wondered about the stranger, was he attached, had he family in these parts children maybe, was he maybe carrying a heavy heart weighed down with the hurt and pain of loss.

Matt was never far from her thoughts.

"I've done an extra bit for your lodger," June left the shepherd's pie on the kitchen table wrapped in a tea towel.

"Be careful, the dish is very hot."

"Aw, sure that young fella. He's as good as any woman in the kitchen," Walter smiled then with a loud sigh he continued,

"I will miss him when he goes."

"He's leaving?" June didn't want to sound too interested.

"Yes. Indeed in I don't know if he knows himself what he wants to do. Same fella doesn't know is he coming or going. Youth, 'tis wasted on the young. Thanks June you're a good girl."

"Something smells good," Matt appeared in the doorway, It was easier now to talk to him, the awkwardness had passed.

"So how's your new boss treating you?" lifting the tea towel Matt took a sniff and smiled, "Yum."

"He's okay, takes a bit of getting used to not having Clodagh around, but it's fine," June turned to walk to the door.

Chapter Twenty-One

"Why don't you stay for dinner, there's plenty."

Walter was setting the table for three as he winked at June. "I'm sure young Matt here would enjoy the company, he's sick of listening to an old codger like me."

They laughed and Matt pulled out a chair for June.

"Madam."

"Poor Lily would be proud of that pie," as Walter got up from the table carrying his plate that he had all but licked clean, he tousled June's hair as he passed.

It put her in mind of the way Pop used to do that, at times she had almost found it annoying, but looking back it had carried a lot of affection. They weren't the hugging and kissing type of people but there were little discreet signs of affection always a feeling of belonging and of course the unspoken but unconditional love.

"'Twould give a man an awful thirst though," and with a wink full of devilment Walter was gone.

"Think he enjoyed that," Matt looked after him as he pulled the door behind him and they both laughed.

"I'll walk you back," Matt folded the tea towel after drying the last plate.

"No, sure I'll be fine. It's only a stone's throw," June reached for her coat.

"I insist," Matt held the door as she closed up her coat.

There was an autumn feel about the night as they walked slowly as if to get the most out of the short journey, they chatted as they went along.

"June, would it be okay if I asked you out one of the nights?"

Matt opened the gate of the cottage, "Just as friends maybe."

June smiled, "That would be nice."

Matt's eyes lit up his feelings for June were the same as ever but he wasn't sure if she felt the same.

These past few weeks they had become friends again but was that just because otherwise it would have been very awkward with him staying at Walter's and June in and out of there all the time!

Perhaps he wasn't sure, he had treated her badly and he still didn't know why he had walked out like that without a word.

It was a rude thing to do, the height of ignorance, he thought to himself, childish behaviour she'd deserved better than that. *Maybe she would give him a chance to make it up to her, maybe, who knows!*

It was eight thirty, Matt would be picking her up at nine and June was like a teenager with butterflies waiting for her first date.

Did the dress make her look frumpy? What if he didn't turn up? What if…?

The doorbell rang.

"I'm a bit early, I know. There's no rush, thought we might go into town and get something to eat." Matt looked so handsome he was wearing a new shirt at least she had never seen it on him before.

"You're fine, I was ready anyway."

Once in each other's company the conversation became easy, the evening was relaxed and fun. June wondered if she should ask Matt in for tea, Matt wondered, if asked should he accept the offer!

"Thanks Matt, I had a lovely time," June opened the gate, she was about to ask him in for tea it was after all the courteous thing to do when Matt put his arms around her and kissed her on the lips.

His eyes filled with tears, "I'm sorry June, I shouldn't have," and he turned to go.

"Matt," June called after him and as he turned 'round she ran to his arms and they kissed so hard that her lips were throbbing after they stopped. The look on Matt's face left no reason for words, they're hearts had spoken.

Chapter Twenty-Two

It was early for the postman but as the card came through the letterbox, June brought her toast with her to see whom it was from.

"Aw, it's Clodagh," she smiled as she read the card aloud.

Matt sitting back in Pop's chair admired her silhouette in the light of the window. Although, she'd always had a sweet tooth and never denied herself a treat, June had the figure of a model, Matt thought, although not one to flaunt it she could give any of those film stars a run for their money.

"Sounds like she's happy," Matt listened as June went on, "she's got her own place, it's a different world out there, she says. Oh! Matt wasn't she great to go."

Reaching for her as she passed him by, Matt took June in his arms and held her.

June giggled as Matt held her tighter when she tried to get up, "So what are your plans?"

Matt wondered was she asking about the day ahead or his future plans. "Only Walter was saying you were talking about moving on, was saying how he'd miss the company," she continued, "And would you miss me June?" Matt had his serious face on now.

June wanted to make light of the moment, "A man's gotta do what a man's gotta do," she smiled.

"I'm late, better run. The keys on the hall table," and she was gone out of the door.

Matt wanted her to say that she would miss him terribly and that he should stay. Maybe he was wrong, maybe they were just friends, but last night!

Malcolm Me Phearson seemed to June like a man with a lot on his mind, as she watched him take stock of the shelves

60

before going to the wholesalers she wondered about his life before he'd taken over the post office.

Was he finding the village life boring? Was he missing the city life he was used to?

It was hard to tell, any conversation they'd had was work related so far and she wasn't one to pry.

"I'll be off then, get ahead of the traffic," he winked at June and was on his way unaware of her thoughts as she watched him go.

He was a very handsome man and not short of a bob or two either, she thought to herself.

"Awful weather out there, goodness I near blew over the quay," Mrs Carey had come through the door puffing and panting, "Wouldn't put a bucket out," she toddled around the grocery shelves talking to her companion, a young boy, *Most likely her grandson*, June thought, as she went round.

"Would want a second pension with the prices they charge these days, daylight robbery."

"Can I help you there Mrs Carey?" June looked over the counter as Mrs Carey replied, "No lovey, I'm grand. I have my little helper today. Sure I'll be only home and I'll think of something else I suppose," walking towards the counter she smiled at June, "A head like a sieve I have."

She went on to talk about her grandson and reading between the lines June could tell she wasn't overly excited about his visit, sounded like he had been a spot of bother.

June had a fear of spiders, Pop used to pick them up and bring them outside, she would scream at the sight of one and watch it until Pop came to take it away just in case she'd lose sight of it.

They moved so fast, if there was one thing worse than a spider in the room it was a missing spider in the room and she wouldn't sleep, she would spend the night watching the walls.

Chapter Twenty-Three

There was no Pop now to call on, she would have to perform the task herself and there wouldn't be any handling or anything like that, it would be squashed and drowned in the toilet, just to be sure to be sure!

June felt a bit of a spring clean coming on, although a couple of seasons too late for a spring clean, by now Nan would be cleaning out the cupboards to make room for the Christmas cakes and puddings that would be baked in the weeks ahead.

She'd always started her Christmas baking in November.

How did those cupboards and drawers get so full of junk. Nan would never have accumulated so much she would bin the lot. Having filled two big black bags with old bits and pieces, June thought, *It is time for a cuppa.*

She picked up a couple of bits of paper she must have dropped on the way to the bin.

"Wondered where that had got to," she smiled as she read Valerie's number and put the piece of paper in her purse, "Never know."

Drinking her coffee, she wondered about Valerie, not enough to ring that number but just what she'd been up to and whether she had ever thought of her.

"Do you think that everyone has a destiny," as they lay in each other's arms Matt spoke gently. The night was fierce outside of the window but with the fire blazing and the scent of the candles the only chill was the one that June felt in her heart at that moment.

"When I went home, June I applied for an American visa," Matt continued in a soft voice, "Rang Mam today and she told me I had post," there was a silence for a moment.

June thought back to when she'd asked Matt to follow his dreams, to do it for her.

Why was it so hard to say it now, she knew this couldn't last, what kind of fool falls in love twice knowing the day would come when they would have to part.

"I think," trying not to choke on her emotion June continued.

"I think given the chance, one should follow their dreams and find their destiny, even if."

Matt held her close, "*Shh*, let's not," he kissed her and with tears in his eyes, "Come with me June."

A moment in time locked in her heart forever.

"Can I leave these with you," Malcolm handed June a box of Christmas decorations. Was it that time of year again?

June thought back to the last time she'd taken down that box with Clodagh, the laughs they had putting up the decorations, "If you'll just have a look through them June, and see if any need replacing or updating," he smiled.

Haven't a clue about these things, June took the box and thought to herself, *they're not the only things needing updating around here*. Earlier she had opened the drawer in her desk and the handle came away in her hand.

The window remained half opened and half closed because it was stuck that way since God knows how long and there was an empty flowerpot left beneath the radiator taking the leak. Malcolm didn't seem to take any interest in the decor, was he just biding his time, would he sell up eventually and make a killing.

June found an angel in the box, Clodagh had been given a present of it for the top of the tree, she was sad suddenly thinking back on the last year. So much had changed so many had moved on, including Matt.

She still missed him but it had been for the best, nothing could ever come of it but that didn't stop her wondering, what if he had been the love of her life? What if she'd never feel that love again? What if she'd gone with him?

But it was Matt's dream not hers!

Chapter Twenty-Four

Christmas bonus week wasn't far off, a busy week at the post office with all the pensioners collecting their bonus.

Many leaving it at the post office to pay off what they owed for bits and pieces they would get on tab.

Malcolm struggled to open the door, both hands loaded with supplies, including new Christmas decorations.

"Might as well push the boat out," he looked very pleased with himself, "might make a start this evening after closing that's if you can spare an hour?"

June smiled, "'Course, no trouble at all."

Doors closed, June started to dust around. *No point decorating over the dust*, she thought to herself.

Mac went up on the stepladder as she handed him the tinsel.

"Not bad for an amateur," he stood back to look when he'd finished, "Thirsty work though, will you join me for a drink or is there somewhere you have to be? I have already taken up enough of your time."

"No, that would be nice," June reached for her coat and Malcolm switched off the lights. They strolled along the quay to Tilly's, the nearest stop not the fanciest of pubs but okay for a drink. He was quite good company, June thought, quite chatty but kept his own business to himself.

There was still another side to him she felt, one he would drift off to every now and then, a sad side!

"Guess we don't really know a lot about each other," as if to read her thoughts Malcolm looked at June enquiringly. "Oh! There isn't much to know," she started to feel uneasy, "This is me this is my world," she wanted to know more about him why wouldn't she ask. She would ask.

It was just making conversation after all.

"It must be a big change for you, I mean the village life when you've been brought up in the city."

He sighed, "Yes, a very big change," his thoughts drifted and his expression changed, "My mother came from these parts," he shook his head and smiled, "bit more complicated than that, but I won't bore you with the details. Let's just say curiosity brought me to these parts initially. Can I get you another drink?"

As he walked to the bar, June watched him, his expensive suit enveloping his muscular body. If she wasn't interested in his background before, she certainly was now, there was definitely something interesting lurking there!

As June searched her bag for the keys of the post office, she promised herself she would clean out that bag the next chance she'd get.

"Morning," Malcolm reached over her shoulder to open the door.

"Hi, never can find anything in this bag."

He smiled but as he put the key in the door he stumbled.

The door was already opened, he looked at June in disbelief.

"I did lock it, didn't I?" and walking slowly through the door his worst fears were realised. He walked hurried towards the locked drawer beneath the counter, the lock had been broken and the drawer emptied.

"I left the money for the Christmas bonus's there."

June was dumbfounded, "What?" She felt for him, in all of her time working there the post office had never before been broken into. Why would he leave so much money lying around, they had only ever left small change in that drawer.

"How much," June was afraid to ask.

"Oh! Why didn't I take it with me? I'm so stupid."

June looked around in shock, whoever had done this knew where to look. Nothing else had been disturbed.

"We'd better call the guards. Let's not touch anything. I'll go to Tilly's and ring."

Chapter Twenty-Five

She ran to the pub down by the quay, although not open for business at this hour she knew Matilda lived over the pub and she would let her use the phone.

Probably would have been okay to use the phone in the post office, she thought to herself, but better to leave things as they were, she arrived at Tilly's breathless.

In thinking about the events of the day later while having a long soak in the bath, June thought of something.

She had been wracking her brain to see if she could remember anyone strange coming into the post office in the few days previous. The guards had taken fingerprints but said it was likely to be someone well known to them who would know their routine.

It was something Mrs Carey had said the few days before that made her think. She'd come into the post office as usual huffing and puffing but she wasn't alone yesterday. She'd had her grandson with her, Rory she had called him, had gotten into a bit of bother at school and was staying with his nan for the few days he'd been suspended for.

She didn't go into detail but June had thought at that moment that there was more to tell, she'd gone on to say she would be in the next few days to collect her Christmas bonus.

June had noticed Rory taking a great interest in the place and would probably have seen her open the drawer to get some change for his nan.

Even if it had been him, and thinking back he would be her first suspect, there was no proof.

Mac had gone to the city it had been three weeks and no word from the guards regarding any developments on the break in.

It was getting very near Christmas now and the evenings were dark and lonely. June remembered a time when she'd thought of the dark evenings as being cosy, curled up on the couch in front of a big roaring fire with Matt.

She wondered if he ever thought of her, there wasn't a day went by that she didn't wonder if she'd made the right decision in staying.

Her days seemed empty, there was something missing.

"Is Mr Mac Phearson about?" a sharp voice called out from the door brought June back to reality.

"Oh come in, no I'm afraid Mr Mac Phearson had to go out for an hour. Can I help?"

The guard took a notebook from his pocket.

"We have a development regarding the break in. Mrs Mac Phearson, is it?"

June smiled. "No, no. I just work here."

The guard didn't seem amused, he was a very straight-faced individual, she thought.

"Would you mind asking Mr Mac Phearson to give me a call when he gets back," handing June a piece of paper on which he had written a phone number he grunted and went on his way. *What a cold person*, June thought.

It turned out there were just the one set of finger prints found, but they'd had nothing on file that matched and would be pursuing the matter further.

"And Mr Mac Phearson was a very foolish man to be leaving that kind of money lying around and maybe he'd learned his lesson."

Mac smiled as he told June on his return from seeing the guard. "Got a right telling off I did, thought he might slap my hand at one stage," they both laughed.

He may very well have learned, but it wasn't a cheap lesson.

June decided not to mention Mrs Carey's grandson, she could have been wrong although she had a feeling she was right but as Pop used to say, "Give him enough rope and sure he'll hang himself, it was only a matter of time before he'd screw up. Can't get away with that for too long!"

Chapter Twenty-Six

The local Community Centre was holding a Christmas party for the old folk on Christmas day. June was asked if she would like to help. Any other Christmas she would donate some pies and treats and that would be that, but this year she thought, *Why not!*

At least, she wouldn't have to spend Christmas alone, well she had intended asking Walter over for Christmas dinner but it wouldn't have been the same with just the two of them.

Poor Walter, never one to complain but would probably have been bored out of his tree. Yes she would join the old folk this year for Christmas dinner and help as well.

"Do I look alright?" Walter stood at June's front door looking like a topper in his báinín jacket, shirt and tie.

"Sure I'd marry you myself," June said as took his arm and walked down the garden path.

There was turkey and ham, and all the trimmings with Christmas pudding and mince pies for afters. There was even a bowl of punch that went down very well as they sat around stuffed and sleepy in the afternoon.

It didn't seem like Christmas at home this year, not without the smell of turkey cooking on the day.

June hadn't bothered to get one, she was never a big fan of turkey but she did miss the lovely Christmas smell.

It had been a lovely day though she had really enjoyed the company. As she walked Walter home, he being ever so slightly tipsy after the punch, they chatted about her nan and pop, and Lily.

"Christmas brings memories of days gone by," Walter had a look of sincerity on his face mixed with sadness, June thought. "She was a wonderful woman, Lily, never known the days to be so long."

June squeezed the old man's arm, thin and frail.

"I know Walter, I know."

There was no more to be said, his face said it all, he would bide his time until the day that they would be re-united again. Although very different circumstances, June could empathise with Walter, she missed Matt.

It was as if she was waiting, waiting for his return, though she knew there would be no return. She had sent him away for God's sake—to follow his dream.

No, there would be no return she was sure of that.

It just felt like she was waiting, couldn't move on in case. Perhaps in her heart she had hoped, even as she had sent him away perhaps she had hoped, he might return, might find that in following his dream, it would lead him back to her! Christmas came and went.

"Time and tide waits for no man," Pop had always said that, there were no truer words.

Mac had invited June to a function held by the wholesalers, a fancy affair by the sounds of it.

"Probably be bored silly but you'd be doing me a big favour," he'd leaned over the counter to ask her. The watery morning sun coming through the window catching the glint in his eyes. She'd hesitated, but just for a moment!

As the doorbell rang, for a split second June thought, What if, what if it was Matt?

Mac held a bunch of crocuses in front of his face as he stood at the door,

"Come in," June blushed as he handed her the flowers, "Thanks Mac, they're lovely." Leaving the vase down on the table, she could feel his eyes on her as she moved. It had been ages since she'd dressed up to go out so she had put in a bit of effort to look good for Mac.

Chapter Twenty-Seven

"You look wonderful," holding her coat for her. *Quite the gentleman*, she thought. Mac was looking with admiration as they walked to the car.

Although never having met any of Mac's friends in the wholesale business, June found them to be a very friendly, jolly bunch.

She'd had a lovely evening. Good food, good company, even had a dance with Mac at the end of the night.

Leaving the taxi running as he walked June to the door, Mac gave her a quick peck on the cheek and thanked her for the lovely evening.

"See you tomorrow."

When inside, June smiled to herself, "Don't need any more complications in my life," she kicked off her shoes with relief. "Why is it that elegant shoes are never comfortable shoes?" and vowed never to wear them again.

Spring was in the air and the garden was coming to life, daffodils appeared through the weeds and June felt nothing but shame for having neglected what was once Nan's pride and joy.

Not a big garden but June remembered the lovely smells in the summer time, Sweet Williams, Wall Flowers, Lilies and in the spring there were Daffodils and Crocuses.

She would take the time to do the garden just as soon as the weather would allow her.

It seemed to have been raining nonstop since Christmas.

Wasn't nature wonderful, she thought, not one bit of attention had she given the daffodils this year and yet there they were an abundance of colour among the weeds.

Cared for by Mother Nature. *Wouldn't want to have been depending on me*, June thought.

Greta had been taken ill, only two doors away June thought she'd make some of Nan's chicken soup to cheer her.

According to Pop there was no better cure for anything from bunions to the plague.

Greta came to the door looking pale and sickly.

"Aw 'tis yourself, come in girl. I'm a bit under the weather."

June closed the door behind her and followed Greta into the kitchen.

"I brought some chicken soup from Nan's old recipe, Nancy was in, told me you were laid up."

"That was very kind of you," Greta had the kettle on the boil without even asking if June would like a cup of tea.

It was an automatic thing when someone called to Greta's house, and one always went home with a few fresh eggs.

The hens were the only income she'd had, supplying the post office with fresh eggs on a daily basis, and sometimes delivering some to the neighbours nearby kept her going.

There was a time when her husband was alive that they would bring their eggs to the market on market day in the city.

"Your nan was a good woman. Wasn't easy taking on an infant at her age, don't know if I could have done it."

Greta noticed the look on June's face and knew she'd said too much.

"I'm sorry June, I shouldn't have said that. My Joe, God be good to him, always said I should think before I speak. Sorry dear, see I went to school with your mother, we were best of friends in those days."

June found it hard to believe that Greta and her mother could be of the same age. She looked so much older than her mother, but then she thought to herself, if one would look closer Greta's grey hair had aged her.

She had quite a young face, June wanted to quiz her about her mother but instead she just assured Greta that there was no offence taken and that Nan had often spoke about things and she agreed that it can't have been easy for her.

Chapter Twenty-Eight

As she took her cup to the sink and made her way to the door, June thanked Greta for the tea and wished her a speedy recovery.

Greta thanked her for the chicken soup and walked her to the door.

"Never could understand what Valerie saw in Roger but they did love each other."

June walked towards the gate as Greta continued, "Himself and Hilda, that was his wife, sure they were like chalk and cheese, complete opposites. She came from a wealthy background, her folks had a business of some sort. Poor Roger, sure he was only living day to day like the rest of us, there was trouble in paradise long before your mother came along."

As she walked back home, June thought about what Greta had said, it can't have been easy she thought what with Nan and Pop getting on and her only a raw infant.

Apart from the shame of it alone, would want great energy to take on a baby at any age June was thinking.

"Did you say there was a cuppa in the pot?" Walter was returning from his Sunday morning stroll after mass.

June just out of bed, hadn't been feeling too well over the weekend, reckoned she'd picked up Greta's bug from her visit earlier on in the week.

She hadn't locked the gate the night before and it had been swinging and banging all through the night with the wind. She'd come out in her dressing gown to close it when Walter passed by.

"Hi Walter, come on in. How are you?"

"Aw, do you know what it is but I'm not the better of seeing young Willie over the road. Ten o'clock on a Sunday morning and he staggering home without a care in the world. Must be out all night. I don't know, and he having a couple of young-uns."

June handed him his tea, "Just a drop of milk and no sugar 'cause you're sweet enough." They both laughed.

As often as she'd served him tea, Walter would still tell her the same thing.

Malcolm Mc Phearson, or Mac as he would say himself had turned out to be a nice enough sort June thought.

Having been working with him now for near on six months, she felt comfortable in his presence.

At first, it seemed strange, she missed Clodagh still.

She wondered how she was getting on, there had only been the one card since she'd gone.

June hoped she was okay she was so brave to just up sticks and go. *Probably busy*, she thought.

The evenings were getting longer and the sun worshippers were again beginning to gather along the quay.

"It's my birthday Friday. Why don't I take my best staff member for dinner to celebrate?" Mac always referred to June as his best staff member when he wanted a favour maybe to work on for an hour or take an awkward phone call or lock up when he wanted to meet friends in the city.

"Your only staff member," June would reply.

"Ya, that would be nice," she knew from a previous conversation that they were around the same age only a year or two in the difference. Mac being the younger.

So she thought to herself, *He must be hitting the thirty mark.*

She wondered about him, never a mention of a girlfriend or going out with anyone. Was none of her business anyway probably wouldn't mention it to her if he was itself.

But why was he celebrating his birthday with a staff member and not his girlfriend!

On her lunch break, June decided to go into town and get something for Malcolm, something small just to mark the occasion. Strolling across the bridge she thought of Valerie, she remembered watching her on that day the first and last time she had met her mother.

Chapter Twenty-Nine

She wondered what she was doing at that time. Was she too strolling around the same shops perhaps thinking about June? The city was busy, June seldom went into town at lunchtime, and it was always the busiest time and seemed to her to be a waste of time when she could stroll in at any time.

Working at the post office gave her the freedom to do that because of her hours there. Didn't pay very much but she was okay financially.

Nan and Pop had left her a place of her own and there were no huge bills as such. June always believed in living within her means Pop had taught her that.

He used to say, "Them lassies with their fancy cars and big houses, sure they must be up to their ears in debt."

June had never learned to drive, neither had she the urge nor the need to drive. The city was within walking distance and sure if she wanted to venture any further there was always the train. The shops were full of bargain hunters with the summer sales on, she didn't want to buy anything personal for Mac. *Maybe a nice bottle of wine*, she thought.

Not that she was any expert on choosing wine but she would ask the assistant for help.

Obviously noticing that June needed help the assistant approached her.

"Any particular taste? Dry, sweet, red white?"

If June was never a wine drinker, she wouldn't be now either after that experience. *The prices they charge for a bottle of wine*, she thought.

Mac looked very handsome in his grey suit, his hair now streaked with grey at the temples was highlighted by his outfit, June thought as she peeped out of the window upstairs when the doorbell rang at seven o' clock on the dot.

"Wow," the expression on Malcolm's face told her she too looked okay and the effort she had put in was worth it.

As they walked to the car, Malcolm held out his arm smiling, "May I?"

They both laughed and the evening turned out to be very enjoyable indeed.

He was lovely company, the awkwardness had passed, they worked well together too and he had always from day one had confidence in June.

Often asking her advice on new lines he was thinking of introducing into the grocery end of things in the post office.

She liked it when he'd consult her about stuff, Clodagh would always include her in her decisions regarding the post office but that was different, Clodagh was like family.

"June, is there, sorry it's…"

June smiled, "Go on."

Mac looked embarrassed, "Is there, well, someone special in your life?"

They had a giggle, "Mac, you don't half get flustered sometimes. No well, not at the moment anyway. There was, but aw sure, that's life isn't it?"

"I'm sorry June, I shouldn't have."

June was a bit curious herself, had been now for a while, "And yourself? Any one special?"

Malcolm went a bright shade of red.

"Long story, but no, no there's no one. Another drink?"

There was an awkwardness for a moment and then Mac went to the bar to call a drink, although June admitted to being stuffed and couldn't manage another drink he insisted he wanted to toast his birthday.

"Another year older," their glasses clashed and as if by impulse Mac reached across the table to kiss June on the lips.

"Happy birthday Mac," June wanted to kick herself for turning away, after all people do kiss on birthdays. Doesn't mean wedding bells!

You fool, she thought to herself, *you old fool.*

76

Chapter Thirty

The car was left in town to be picked up the following day because Mac had been drinking and it being a lovely moonlit night they decided to walk back.

"Be good to walk off some of that meringue pie."

June had created an awful embarrassing moment at the table and felt bad about it.

"Mac, I'm sorry. I don't know why I do things sometimes. Sorry"

"That's okay, June. Probably too much wine. Forget it."

The town was alive with people of all ages out enjoying the night.

June didn't often go into town at night and as she walked through the crowds and the buzz of people around she promised herself that she would make an effort and go out more.

As if!

Mrs Sheridan was standing at her gate. *It is late*, June thought, *for her to be standing there.*

"Goodnight Mrs Sheridan," June spoke gently so as not to startle her as they approached.

"Oh, goodnight dear. Cheeky's gone missing."

Cheeky was Mrs Sheridan's cat, she'd found him one morning in the garden covered in snow, she doted on him.

Her husband had been putting out the bin when he'd noticed the movement in the garden. She must have huddled up out of the cold and gotten covered by a fall of snow.

"We'd thought of naming her Snowy," Mrs Sheridan continued, "on account of where she'd turned up, but she had such a cheeky look in her eyes we thought Cheeky suited her better. I wonder where she has gone."

Although making light of the situation, June could see that Mrs Sheridan was indeed concerned, "Don't worry she won't have gone far, she'll turn up," and just as June had the words out of her mouth along came Cheeky.

"Where on earth have you been?" Her eyes alight with gladness, Mrs Sheridan cuddled her cat and bid them goodnight.

"Aren't folk around here lovely?" Malcom opened the gate as they approached June's house, "Sort of, I don't know, homely. Don't get much of that anymore, least not where I come from."

June hoped she wasn't being presumptuous in inviting Mac in for tea but it seemed the right thing to do.

As she filled the kettle, she watched as he strolled around the kitchen looking at old photographs on the mantle and taking one in his hand.

"Are those your folks?"

"That's my nan and pop, they've both passed on now. They were the best."

"And your parents?" Mac noticed the change in June's expression.

"Sorry June, just when you said."

"It's okay. My nan and pop reared me. My mother left when I was very young. Long story. Tea or coffee?"

June wasn't about to spoil a lovely evening talking about her own misfortunes. *Not that he'd be the least bit interested anyway*, she thought to herself.

They chatted for ages then Mac got up and took his coffee cup to the sink.

"Never realised the time. Best be on my way."

As they walked to the door, Mac thanked June for accompanying him and gave her a quick peck on the cheek.

Climbing the stairs June didn't really feel tired she'd had a lovely evening, she thought how she had got into a rut didn't do anything very exciting anymore. Was Matt's memory going to spoil her chances of ever finding happiness again? Maybe you do only get one chance of happiness!

Chapter Thirty-One

The church barbeque was to be held the previous week but was cancelled on account of the bad weather promised, so it would go ahead this Sunday weather permitting.

There were flags and bunting out and bells ringing in the ears of the poor saints with prayers to bring fine weather.

It brought a great crowd, with local produce on sale from cakes and buns to fresh eggs and home-grown vegetables, and saints be praised there wasn't a drop of rain or a cloud to be seen in the sky.

"Can't be doing with that, what do they call it, barbequing is it would burn the mouth off you," Walter was drinking water by the gallons, "By golly 'tis hot stuff."

June had to laugh as he walked by huffing and puffing.

"It was indeed a great turn out," Father Mulcahy had said as he thanked everyone concerned from the alter, the following Sunday at mass. Not forgetting to thank the wonderful saints for sending the fine weather and he hoped it would continue for the rest of the summer.

"I was thinking of going home for a few days, do you think you could manage? Or would you like me to get an extra hand in for a few days?"

June was cashing up, it was pension day and one of the busiest for a while, "I'll be fine."

Mac walked across to where she was sitting and sat on her desk, "You sure? Some business to sort out at home. I'll go Monday and be back on Friday."

"That's grand." June had been on her own lots of times, she'd be fine.

"June, would you be kind enough to put that in the window for me lovey?" Mrs Beatty handed June a card that read, 'Sum of money lost. Please contact'.

"Oh Mrs Beatty, not your pension surely?" June remembered her signing for her pension at the counter the day before.

"Yes lovey, I went straight home. Must have lost it out of my shopping bag. Sure maybe someone that needs it more than me found it."

The hairdressing salon in the village had been run by Mrs Sheridan for years.

Had retired now and closed up of course but you could still get that smell of perm solution as you walked past.

June remembered going in there as a child with her nan, she would have her hair permed every spring without fail.

Said the set would last longer if she'd had the perm in, she would set it herself the rest of the time.

The visit to the hairdressers was a luxury she could only afford on an annual basis.

June had been blessed with her own natural curls Nan would say, though at times, June would say she'd been cursed she dreaded the weekly washing of her long curly hair back then, the tangles and the tears!

And sure if there was a bit of a mist in the air at all she'd have a halo around her face.

Mac didn't seem the same when he returned from his business meeting at home, seemed very into himself, as if deep in thought. June wondered if maybe business wasn't going so well, perhaps he was contemplating selling up and moving back home into the family business.

She wouldn't dare to ask him what was on his mind, but there was definitely something bothering him.

She would wait if it concerned the post office and her she would hear all in good time.

Summer now coming to an end, there was a feel of autumn in the air, a chill in the mornings.

Chapter Thirty-Two

Walking past the store where they had met, seemed a lifetime ago now but June's thoughts once again drifted back to Matt, she wondered what he might be doing. If he ever thought of her!

It had rained all day, there were puddles everywhere and a strong wind blowing.

"Better watch the tides tonight, with that wind it could come up."

Walter tucked his pension book under his top coat as he opened the post office door and looked back, 'High tides promised'.

Poor Walter was so caring, June had never known a couple as close as him and Lily, he must miss her dreadfully.

The evenings getting darker now and the mornings too, June enjoyed her little lie in on a Sunday morning went to the last morning mass and strolled along the quay afterwards. Perhaps it was the sound of the water that calmed her but it always made her feel better to be near to the sea.

Clodagh came to mind, she wondered how she was getting on, she'd only had one card since she'd left and no return address so that keeping in contact was impossible.

Clodagh had mentioned that she would probably have to move around from place to place, wherever she was needed and there was no point in trying to get in contact, but she did promise to keep in touch.

Things were so different back then when Clodagh was around.

Seemed a long time ago now but it wasn't really.

Mac was a gentleman to work for and June would never say a bad word about him, but working with Clodagh was lovely. They'd share the joys and the miseries of the weekend on a Monday morning and have a giggle at a painful customer, just silly things but June missed it.

"I found it! June, I found it!" Mrs Beatty came running across the road from the chapel.

"Sure I hadn't put it down in my bag at all, didn't I put it in my apron pocket inside in my coat? I never thought about it until I put it in the wash, it was then that I checked the pockets and there it was. I think I might have given poor St Anthony a headache," and seeing her neighbour coming out of the chapel Mrs Beatty took off as fast as she arrived laughing and shouting, "I found it Mrs Kelly, I found it!"

Running late the next day June found that the post office was already open when she got to work ten minutes late.

"I'm so sorry Mac, I didn't realise the time."

"Will you stop? Sure aren't you here every morning to open up you're grand."

Mac was going through the post, "Good weekend?"

"Aw, the usual," June replied as she hung her coat on the back of the door, "Nothing too exciting, and you?"

They both laughed, "Same here, how sad are we, eh?" Mac went back to sorting his post as June took up her usual place behind the desk.

"We'd be thirty years wed today if poor Lily, God be good to her, were alive."

June had gone round to Walter's with a bit of dinner.

"Oh Walter, I had no idea," not usually stuck for words June didn't know what to say.

"Aw sure we had many a good year, I can't complain."

Lily would have been so proud of Walter, he'd missed her terribly but had soldiered on kept the house spick and span dusted all of her treasures on the mantle on a regular basis.

He knew she had taken such pride in her home that she wouldn't want it any other way.

The clock ticked loudly and other than the kettle on the boil there wasn't another sound. It must have been so lonely for him at times although having said that Walter did go out and about a lot.

Chapter Thirty-Three

As he shuffled around the kitchen, June thought he'd begun to look frail, she hadn't noticed before but then Walter was getting on now too. *Must be nearing the eighty mark*, she thought, he was an active enough man for his age and as he'd say himself he can't complain.

She would wait and have a cup of tea with him, chat for a little while she remembered Nan used to say, "Take the time to talk, if anything should wait let the work wait." Maybe she was right, sometimes it's enough just being there.

"Lily was my second wife you know June?" Walter had taken her by surprise, she hadn't realised.

"No, I didn't know that Walter."

"Was a long time before I moved here, long before I met Lily. We were very young, a lifetime ago."

June put the milk and sugar in her tea, had tried to give up the sugar but that didn't last long.

"We were nineteen, the first girl I ever went out with. Used to take her fishing you know. Aw, she was a bonny girl, were only three years married when I lost her."

June listened in awe.

"That was hard. Time steals June, Time steals."

Seems Margaret, his first wife had been very delicate as a child. They'd grown up together she'd suffered with cystic fibrosis. "There was nothing back then, not like there would be now," Walter said, she loved life.

Her condition didn't get in the way, they used to go fishing and camp out under the stars on summer evenings.

It was hard to imagine Walter young and full of adventure perhaps it was true, what he said, life steals. June only ever remembered him as old Walter.

Margaret had taken ill while he was out on a fishing trip, there was no way of contacting him only to have someone meet him on his return it had been too late, she had gone when he'd got back.

"She loved marigolds. Funny, so many beautiful flowers to choose from, yet she loved the humble marigold."

Walter went on to talk about Lily, he'd been alone for many years after losing Margaret before he met Lily.

They'd met on the train, Lily was returning from the city after a day trip and Walter was contemplating moving to the seaside, maybe get back into the fishing again. After he'd lost Margaret, he couldn't bear to go back to the fishing for a long time.

Blamed the sea for his not making it back on time to be there for her. So much bitterness eats you up inside he'd said so he wanted a change of scenery, a fresh start.

They'd got to talking on the train and as it happened Lily's mother had run a boarding house by the quay.

He worked as a handy man about the place for his board and meals and put a bit aside to eventually get his own boat and make a living once again from the sea. At the end of the day, it was where he was happiest.

Somehow he and Lily got thrown together, maybe it was fate maybe it was convenience, he wasn't sure but they grew very fond of each other and he asked her to marry him.

A bit long in the tooth for love at first sight, he called it a comfortable friendship that grew into a trusting and loving relationship.

"Ouch," as often as she had closed that drawer June never failed to catch her finger in it.

"You okay?" Mac was heading to the wholesalers for the monthly stock.

"I'm fine, no stranger to pain, me," they both laughed as he closed the door behind him.

"Be with you in a moment," June on hearing the post office door open got up from under the counter where she had attempted to repair the drawer unsuccessfully of course!

Chapter Thirty-Four

"Clodagh!" she screamed at the top of her voice to see her friend standing there, "It's so good to see you."

"You too!" Clodagh took a minute to look around what was once her empire, '

"Where's Mac?"

"He's just stepped out to the wholesalers."

"Business is good."

"Ya."

Looking at Clodagh, June thought she looked tired probably up all night travelling, bound to be tired sure.

"You back for good?" just as she had the words out of her mouth the door opened.

Clodagh walked around the counter taking everything in as she went, as if reminiscing.

The customer looked after, June turned her attention back to her friend who had now sat in her old chair behind Mac's desk.

"It's like a lifetime ago, so much has happened," Clodagh smiled.

"You're back for good?," June was eager to know how things went so many questions so much she wanted to ask.

"Maybe we can meet later, tell you all about my travels."

"Come round for dinner," June knew the post office wasn't exactly the ideal place to have a chat, not with people coming in and out every five minutes.

"That would be lovely," Clodagh agreed to call at seven and June spent the afternoon deciding what she would cook. *Nothing too complicated*, she thought, *something handy!*

Sitting and chatting like old times, June could see the tears in Clodagh's eyes as she spoke about the conditions people lived in out where she was a volunteer.

"So much sickness, no medication to speak of," Clodagh went on to talk for hours, just realising the time she got up to go. "Thanks June, I needed that."

June was so mad with her booking a place to stay in town when she could have stayed with her. Wasn't the Ritz or anything like it but she could have stayed, it would have been lovely to have her, she thought as she waved her goodbye at the door.

"Had a better offer then," Mac was already in when June got to the post office the next morning. For a moment, she hadn't a bull's notion of what he was talking about.

Then it clicked, he had asked her for a drink in Tilly's after work the evening before as he went off to the wholesalers. In the meantime, Clodagh had turned up and sure with all the excitement of seeing her old friend again and rushing home to get the tea ready June just plain forgot about Tilly's and Mac! "Sorry Mac, Clodagh arrived home unexpectedly and it just went out of my head."

"Not to worry, how is Clodagh? Still doing her volunteering bit?"

June wasn't entirely sure if Mac was being sarcastic or really interested in how Clodagh was getting on, he seemed just a bit, well she wasn't sure what but he wouldn't know Clodagh well enough, in her books, to comment on how she choose to spend her time.

June longed for the bright evenings, it seemed she was going to work in the dark and coming home in the dark these days.

The only bit of daylight she was seeing was her twenty minutes lunchtime, if it was a fine day she would take a stroll just to get a bit of fresh air.

Clodagh's two weeks at home had passed all too quickly, it was her last night and June wanted to take her somewhere nice, she would ask Mac to join them, it would be nice for them to meet again.

"That was just delicious," Clodagh held her glass up to propose a toast, "To old friends."

Mac smiled and replied, "And not so old," they all laughed.

Chapter Thirty-Five

Walking her back home after saying their farewells to Clodagh, as her flight was very early the next morning, Mac looked puzzled as he asked June, "What do you think of Clodagh? I mean no money, worries, not a care in the world. Her own little business. Why would she want to go traipsing across the world like that? Is it a calling? What do you think?"

"I don't know, maybe, I just think people who do that sort of thing are great. They're so selfless, so concerned for others. I don't know."

Mac didn't say another word on the subject.

They walked for a while in silence then Mac putting his arm around June's shoulder. *More for support*, she thought, *than anything else.*

"So what about you? Anyone special in your life?"

June smiled, "I think we had better get you home Mr Mac Phearson."

"You're not bringing me in for coffee?"

You need coffee alright, June thought to herself, *black and plenty of it*.

Mac stumbled as he went in the front door, fell to the ground and brought June with him in the process, they both laughed.

You'll be well embarrassed over this on Monday, she thought to herself, *well embarrassed.*

Eventually getting him off the floor she plonked him in the nearest chair and went to put the kettle on, though she knew in her heart and soul that he hadn't a notion of drinking coffee, he was asleep already, and she would leave him to sleep it off.

She was right, Mac apologised for a full week after and even still every now and then, he would bring it up.

"I'm a pint man myself, don't usually drink wine. Must have gone to my head. I was fine at the table, just when we got outside. Wow. I'm sorry June. Did I say anything stupid?"

The first letter from Clodagh arrived about six weeks after she'd gone back to Africa, she was well but finding it harder to settle back than she'd expected but she would be fine after a while. She'd commented on Mac and how she'd noticed a sort of chemistry between him and June that night at dinner.

June was gob smacked, there was no such thing nor would there ever be and she would put her friend right in the next letter, she was so glad Clodagh had included a return address this time.

The weather had turned very cold overnight, June wanted to visit Nan and Pop's grave, she would make up a nice winter basket. The ground would be too cold to plant but the basket would be nice, winter pansies maybe.

"Plenty of room for you here," Nan, poor soul would say as they walked away from Pop's grave. She would hold June's hand so tightly as they walked away her fingers would go numb and white. Hail, rain or snow they would go up there every Sunday after mass. *Not so now*, June thought.

It had been a while what with work and all she would console herself knowing full well there was absolutely no excuse in the world apart from the fact that she hated the place.

The thought of being buried in the clay gave her the creeps, spiders and whatnot!

June missed them both so much, she could still hear Nan pottering around the kitchen, would ask if you were okay sometimes and by the time you would turn to answer sure she had gone polishing some other corner muttering away to herself, "Sure yer grand, isn't it well for ya, being young."

Growing up in Nan and Pop's house, being reared as their own was something June would be eternally grateful for.

Now, had Valerie stayed around who knows it might have worked out okay too but there was something about the older generation. They always had time, something nowadays seemed a rarity, people are always rushing, about June thought including herself. In Nan's time, it was more important to sit and have a chat.

Chapter Thirty-Six

June had promised herself a long time ago that she too would give her children time, that's if she ever had children of course, a possibility that was beginning to look bleaker by the minute these days, her clock was ticking very loud, very loud indeed.

She remembered Pop used to say,

"Que será, será. Whatever will be, will be."

She too believed that, "What was for ya, wouldn't go by ya," a great old saying of her old pop. Even after all this time, she still missed them.

Mrs Carey, usually a friendly bubbly woman, today seemed very quiet, not herself at all.

June watched as she folded her pension neatly into her purse with a worried look on her face. She'd known Mrs Carey for a long time now. "Betty," she would often say, "My name is Betty, don't be calling me Mrs Carey," as June always called her in handing her the pension.

June wasn't one to pry, but she did seem awfully sad not at all her usual self. "Are you okay, Mrs Carey?" she put her arm around her shoulder, a frail little woman but very hardy always.

"It's a curse," she said with a shake in her voice, "Money. 'Tis a curse girl," June didn't know what to say, was she having a hard time keeping up with the bills? Would she offer to help her out?

She didn't want to insult her at the same time but she had to do something. She brought Mrs Carey into the back room, it was about time to close up anyway.

That was another thing that was completely out of character with her today she was always in to collect her pension first thing, she was the last customer today!

Mac had gone on another of his business trips, seemed to go off like that a lot lately, June wasn't sure if she should be worried about this or not but today she was concerned about Mrs Carey, she would think about that another day.

"Thanks June. You're a very kind girl," June smiled and offered Mrs Carey a chocolate biscuit to go with her tea.

"I don't mean to pry Mrs Carey, but you were so upset. Is there anything I can do to help you out, a few pounds maybe?"

Mrs Carey smiling now among the tears replied, "Oh my dear, you are so kind. If only, that was the problem. Sure I will never live to spend what our Ollie left to me when he passed on."

Ollie it seemed was a brother of Mrs Carey's that worked all of his life in America and never married, came home a couple of years earlier to die and left a small fortune to his only sister, Mrs Carey.

"No lovey," Mrs Carey continued, "It's far worse than being short a few bob I'm afraid, far worse. My heart is broken girl. My heart is broken."

As June listened to this frail old lady speak of the shame of her grandson being involved in a robbery, she thought to herself, she was not missing out on having teenagers in this world.

"You see," Mrs Carey continued, "I suppose the signs were there, that's what's breaking my heart. Maybe if we had done something earlier, maybe."

She went on to say that for a while now things had been going missing in the house, little things, but eventually she realised it was always when her grandson had stayed over.

They lived a bit away and whenever her daughter worked late (she was nursing) she would ask Mrs Carey to have her grandson to stay over. Her daughter didn't like to leave him on his own since his dad had long since gone.

A long story she'd said her daughter had given him the door.

Not going into too much detail, June suspected they had parted on bad terms, reading between the lines and judging by the look on Mrs Carey's face.

"You don't like to accuse anyone, ya know? My goodness especially not one of your own, and he was so well reared that fella. Never wanted for anything. Sure he only had to ask," Mrs Carey having settled a bit by now, got up to leave.

"I'm sorry June, I'm holding you up," June assured her it was no bother at all.

Chapter Thirty-Seven

"You know," turning back as she went to the door Mrs Carey still with tears in her eyes continued, "I did ask him once, when money had gone missing on me, had he taken it. Now I knew he had to have because apart from myself there was no one else in the house. Unless it was the fairies," she sort of smiled, "June he convinced me that he didn't take it. He was so convincing that you would have to believe him. It scared me."

"I suppose I should have told his mother then but it's a very hard thing to do to accuse your own, very hard indeed. They're all I have in the world, I didn't want to be falling out with them."

She was indeed heartbroken, June thought to herself as she locked the door behind her, wished her well and told her to try not to worry too much.

On top of it all then, she was feeling guilty that maybe if she had told her daughter about her suspicions she might have nipped it in the bud and avoided his getting into worse trouble.

Now he was serving six months in a correction centre, locked up at fourteen years of age. *What kind of future would come out of that experience*, June thought.

In her time, a good clip round the ear would put an awful quick stop to any wrongdoing and you wouldn't do it a second time either.

Why should this poor old woman suffer with her conscience over a grandson who, if he ever had an ounce of affection or respect for the woman, wouldn't do that to her in the first place.

There was something awfully wrong there.

June thought, she pitied the woman but there wasn't a blessed thing she could do to help her, it is very hard to see the bad in someone you love.

She remembered Matt talking about his mother, how she had suffered at the hands of his father through drink and violence and yet she'd stayed with him scarred both physically and mentally. *We are a very weak species*, June thought, *when it comes to affairs of the heart.*

She wondered how Matt's mother was these days, and she wondered about Matt.

June heard the screech of breaks and ran to the window, she'd been tidying out the old wardrobes in Nan and Pop's room putting the best of what she'd found in bags for charity.

Some of Pop's clothes still with the tags on, dear old Pop never one for style but every birthday and Christmas Nan would buy him a new shirt and a cardigan without fail and only the best would do.

Paid through the nose for them too, she wasn't one for the city, did all her shopping in the drapers down the road.

Sure Pop would tell her not to be buying for him, "Who's going to be looking at an old codger like me?" he would say opening the parcel and winking at June.

June remembered picking daisies in the field with her pop and giving them to her nan on her birthday, that was many moons ago now, couldn't recall ever giving Pop a present but she must have she thought.

It was the milkman that had screeched on his brakes outside, a woman was stood in the middle of the road but from the window, June couldn't make out who it was or what had happened, she would run and see if she could be of any help.

By now a small crowd had gathered, it was Mrs Beatty, she'd walked right out in front of him the driver said, "Couldn't avoid her," he was very shaken he took his jacket and folded it under her head.

She was pale as death and trembling but at least she was alive June thought, she could have been killed.

Nancy was still standing in the middle of the road, June took her by the arm and led her onto the path.

"My God, June, is she dead?"

Chapter Thirty-Eight

June taking a trembling Nancy to a nearby window sill to sit her down, told her not to fret and that everything would be all right. Someone had rung for an ambulance from Tilly's and it would be there shortly.

Not sure herself, if everything would be fine, June hoped she was right but for the moment it was a bit of consolation for the poor woman's friend who had just been chatting to her outside the church after mass.

"I should go and get Mr Father Mulcahy," Nancy had up and gone before June could answer.

Going about their business in such a professional manner June watched as the ambulance men took such care in moving Mrs Beatty, they seemed to put her at ease straight away. Still well shook looking but more at ease, she held her hand to her head as they carried her to the ambulance on a stretcher.

News of her condition wasn't so good as it came after a few days, she had injured her spine and would not walk again, a few short moments and your life is changed forever!

Walter was in a state as he went on to tell June what he had heard, "My good God, that poor woman."

Mac looked shattered as he returned from yet another business trip, June thought. She wanted to ask him if everything was okay, she didn't know what was wrong but his face was full of sadness sometimes, a look of loss in his eyes.

Not the type to talk about his private life, June decided she would leave well alone and get on with her work.

There was certainly a mystery behind this man!

"June, could I ask you something?"

Had he read her thoughts, maybe caught her looking at him "Yes, of course. What is it? Everything okay?"

continuing to pack the cigarettes on the shelf as if only mildly interested (as if) she was only dying to hear what he had to say.

"Did you ever know a man called Roger Atkins around these parts?"

Shrugging her shoulders June replied, "No, name doesn't ring a bell. Should I?"

Mac now sitting on the counter twisting his keys around his finger, "No, doesn't matter. Listen you doing anything later? Fancy a drink at Tilly's?"

Agreeing to meet her there Mac jumped off the counter and was gone out the door, one of these days, June thought to herself, *that counter is going to give!*

'Roger Atkins', never heard any mention of anyone of that name around these parts, she thought and sighed as she locked up to go home, another day over.

Tilly's was quiet for a Saturday night, had Mac not asked her to meet him she would be tucked in beside the fire herself she thought, it was a miserable night for the fire and a good book.

"Quiet here isn't it?" Mac got up to get a drink when June arrived.

It was cosy though, a nice turf fire and candles on the table, not ever a busy pub, Tilly's was a place to have a drink before one would hit the town for a night out, but June liked it.

A little old fashioned compared to some in town but always welcoming and sort of homely.

Turned out to be a good night, quite enjoyable. Had a few laughs and as Mac walked her home June thought he was in better form much more relaxed than earlier. *But that could be the drink too*, she thought.

Putting the kettle on for a cup of tea, June was chatting to Mac who had now strolled over to Pop's old chair to make himself comfortable.

"Tea or coffee?"

Must have nodded off, she thought when she didn't get an answer, taking the tea to the table she was stopped in her stride as she noticed Mac with his head in his hands, bent over in Pop's chair. "Mac? Are you okay? Mac?"

Chapter Thirty-Nine

Without opening his eyes, he held her as she knelt on the floor beside him and sobbed and sobbed, after what seemed like an eternity he sat up and had a sip of tea, "I'm sorry June, it's such a mess."

Maybe she would just sit there and he would eventually talk, she didn't want to pry.

"Mac. If there's anything I can do," she asked emphatically. Holding her hand, the tears still wet on his face Mac nodded and got up to go.

Turning round at the front door, he hugged her so tight that she wanted to cry herself.

"Come back inside Mac, talk to me please."

Mac sat on the stairs inside the door, he had sobered up very quickly, June's heart was breaking looking at him but she had to keep a face on.

"I was married, June. Oh, it was seven years ago now. We were very happy. Thought we were together for life," pausing for a moment he continued, "to make a long story short, we went on holiday, made up a foursome with a good mate of mine and his girlfriend—current girlfriend," he paused again. This time his face filled with anger. Turned out his wife, Freda, had been seeing this 'good mate' of his for months after they returned from holiday, was his now ex-girlfriend that enlightened him.

"Stupid, naive, idiot that I am I never spotted it. Never spotted it, June. It was going on in front of my eyes and I never spotted it."

"I'm so sorry Mac." *What do you say,* June thought.

They had split up and hadn't had any contact since, Mac had bumped into a friend of Freda's while in town a while back and she had told him of Freda's situation.

She had moved in with her new-found love only to find that within a couple of months he'd had another fancy piece in tow.

"I know she's no longer my concern, but it's hard, you know. She's in a bad way it seems, drinking, late bars, bad company."

Putting her arm around his shoulder, June thought to herself, *He still loves this girl*, then out of the blue he kissed her.

It was a very passionate kiss, she was aware he was in a very vulnerable state and she was merely a shoulder to cry on.

He'd talked and talked through the early hours.

As she watched him go, June thought to herself, *Freda, you fool, some people don't realise when they have it good.*

He was a fine man, and he really loved that girl.

After Matt, June had told herself she was better off out of the relationships department and she was beginning to think she was right, though there were days when she took some convincing, life on your own could be lonely at times. Love for all its ups and downs made you feel alive, a part of something. There were days when she longed for that and then there were days when she was just grand.

"Morning June," Mrs Mac closed the door behind her, "Goodness, would skin a cow out there today."

It had turned very cold over the last couple of days.

"Just passed by the chapel there was a squad car outside. Strange, right up to the front door too it was."

June so enjoyed the little chats with the folk round here, nosey as hell some of them but all in good nature.

"Hope there's no one taken ill or anything now. Keep telling poor old Nancy there. Sure there's no need for her to be running down to mass these mornings and her not hardly able to walk sure. What sin is on her? What sin is on any of us for that matter, all we want is to be able to look back and have no regrets as they say, isn't that all," disappearing behind the freezer department Mrs Mac was still chatting away and not a sinner listening to her.

Chapter Forty

Christmas came and went, weeks of hustle and bustle, community get-togethers, decorations, buying in supplies like there was going to be a famine, and cold, cold mornings.

Icicles hanging in places June had never seen icicles hang before, there was obviously a leak in the ceiling over the door in the post office, there had to be water surely for icicles to form! It was the coldest winter she could remember.

"Hi Walter."

With his head hung low Walter took his cap off and handed June a letter, "Come in. What's up, what's this?"

"'Tis bad news, June, terrible news."

Taking his cap she guided him to the chair, he seemed somewhat disorientated.

"'Tis young Matt, he's gone June. Killed crossing the road only weeks after he left it seems. 'Tis all there in the letter."

June felt numb, "What. Oh my God. It can't be."

Still holding the letter in her hand, she found herself sitting on the stairs, not remembering how her legs carried her there.

They talked for hours, seemed Matt's mother had found Walter's address in Matt's belongings that had been posted on to her by his landlady after his death.

Full of compassion and empathy towards Matt's family. She seemed a very kind lady, Matt's mother thought.

Seems he'd just found himself a job and was staying with another lad sharing a room, the landlady had said hoping to make it in the big city.

She'd had a letter from him the week previous, with his usual concern of her situation at home, hoping everything was okay. The awful news had come to her by phone, she said she'd realised when she heard the American accent on the phone that something was up, she'd hoped he hadn't got into trouble, but never expected to hear what she was about to hear.

His travel insurance had paid for the cost of bringing him home to them, otherwise Matt would have been buried among strangers.

On their income, it would have been out of their reach financially to bring him home.

The whole village had turned out to support them in their loss, but Matt's dad had taken to the drink, this time to be the cause of him getting a stroke and losing his walk.

It had taken her all this time to come to terms with writing this on paper, she had made many attempts, she knew Walter had been a good friend to Matt and he had a right to know, she still had many very bad days.

Matt had mentioned a girl a couple of times before he'd left for America and she'd wondered if maybe Walter knew anything about her, she had never known Matt to talk about a girl before so she reckoned she must have been kinda special to him.

"Its awful news to have to tell anyone," she wrote but she should know too.

Seems there was a letter in his belongings addressed to Walter but never got posted, she would post this to him in the near future, thought it would be best that he would hear of the tragedy first and come to terms with it.

Matt had died instantly, the voice on the phone had said, he didn't suffer.

If that was to be a consolation, it didn't console.

"My God," June looked across the table to where Walter was sitting. He looked old and shattered, she thought.

Taking his handkerchief out of his pocket, he blew his nose. "Wouldn't have made a bit of difference."

June couldn't get her head around this.

"What wouldn't make a bit of difference, Walter?"

"If you had gone with him, if he had stayed. Wouldn't make a bit of difference a girl. His time was up. That was that.

104

Poor lad, and he just starting out in life and there's me an old codger, no good to anyone."

June felt numb, angry, confused, she didn't know what she was feeling and she felt for poor Walter, he was terribly upset too.

Chapter Forty-One

"Stop now Walter. That's not true. Stop now."

They sat in silence for what seemed like an age, she wondered about Matt's parents, should she go visit them, would that be okay, would it be the right thing to do?

God she didn't know what to do, she just felt numb.

Matt was the love of her life, she felt so alone, she wished Nan was there.

As Walter got up to go, he staggered,

"I'm grand," he said.

"The old sticks aren't what they used to be."

Walking out the pathway he stopped for a moment and looked back at June, "Ya know, you need to grab any happiness in this world grab it with both hands. You only get one chance. One chance girl, we know not the hour nor the day."

A few words on paper, she had read it over and over again.

Would it ever sink in, would it ever stop hurting, a few life changing words.

She would never love anyone in the way she'd loved Matt. Sitting on the bus June hoped she was doing the right thing, Walter wasn't sure if going to visit Matt's parents was a good idea, she would have to decide for herself, he'd said but he was sure they would be nice people.

"Matt was a nice fella and the apple don't fall far from the tree," Walter gave her a wink and wished her luck.

She thought of Matt and how he'd hated the bus journey home, "Every mile is a mile further away from where my heart is," he would say and they'd hug so tight that she would have to catch her breath, the bus would only be gone around the corner and she would be missing him already.

Why did she ever let him go, she'd wanted him to be truly happy and that meant to follow his dream.

"That's why," she'd told herself, she'd hoped one day that the love she knew he'd felt for her might bring him back to her.

She had wanted him to stay so badly, but it had to be his own decision if it was to be right, if it was to last.

Perhaps that was his intention, perhaps he was crossing the road to book his flight home because he'd missed her so much and he was going to surprise her on the doorstep. Perhaps, he had realised in following his dreams that they had led him back to her, but now she would never know.

The bus came to a sudden halt and brought June's thoughts back to reality, it was a farmer taking his cattle across the road, seemed to take for ages but she didn't mind, she still didn't know if she was doing the right thing.

Matt had asked her to go with him the last time he went to visit his parents but she didn't, she remembered he'd said that the bus stopped at the corner shop and he would get out there, it was only a stone's throw from the home house.

Not knowing in what direction to go from the corner shop, June decided to go in and ask the assistant if she knew the family.

"Aw sure, that poor woman. Young Matt did a paper round for me in his younger days, a smashing lad. Always so obliging and always with a smile on his little face. God help us he had such dreams, even as a youngster."

Only too eager to help, she pointed June in the right direction and off she went. Feeling a bit apprehensive on approaching the gate, she continued on up the path to the door, before she got a chance to knock the door opened.

A frail old lady stood there, on looking closer June saw that she wasn't quite that old but aged and weary looking.

"Heard the gate, thought it was our nurse. Are you new in the area?"

June smiled, there was no mistaking this lady was Matt's mother, same kind eyes, a great resemblance.

Chapter Forty-Two

"No I'm," June struggled not to burst into tears, as the puzzled lady looked on.

"I'm June, I knew your son, Matt."

As she watched this lady's curiosity turn to sadness, June wasn't sure she had done the right thing at all in coming,

"I'm so sorry. I should go."

She turned to go as Matt's mother wiped her tears away, "No dear. It's me that's sorry, come in, come in dear," a very cosy little house, clean and tidy.

In need of some repair no doubt, but as she pottered round her little kitchen June could see that her home was her pride and joy. There was no awkwardness in their talking, it was like talking to an old friend.

Matt had so many of his mother's traits and ways of speaking.

It was obvious he had been her world.

They talked for ages with no mention of what was Matt's biggest worry in life, the abuse his mother suffered at the hands of his father.

Now bed ridden due to ill health his father had a daily nurse calling, his mother had thought that June had been his nurse calling as she was due any minute.

She would fix him up and be off again.

For the rest of the time, Matt's mother would care for him herself, her eyes bore no resentment towards the man who had made her life so miserable, drinking what little he earned and when that had run out, taking it out on her.

Yet there was only love in her eyes as she spoke of him and pity for his now ill health.

What kind of love is this, June thought to herself, *what is it that makes a person stay where abuse and neglect take away their self-respect and reduce their confidence to where they merely exist, to such a low that they accept what they know is so wrong.*

"You know," Matt's mother went on. "I had never known our Matt to speak about a girl before he spoke about you, he was always the shy type. Said he'd met someone last time he came to visit, said time would tell. I think you were very special to him, I could tell."

As she spoke about him, she had such a sadness in her eyes, almost as if she had lost everything, as if all she had, had been taken from her.

"I was so blessed for that short time I had him," she went on… "so blessed…"

"You know June, Matt worked so hard to save for that boat it was his pride and joy. I knew it would mean losing him to the sea eventually of course, but if it brought him happiness well sure isn't that all you can hope for in this world—a little bit of happiness," as she looked across the room to the window she continued.

"America, always hoped it was just him letting off steam. He got frustrated at times. His dad and him never saw eye to eye, but his dad loved him as much as I did, just, aw sure," she got up from the table, "more tea?"

June would have loved to chat some more but her bus was due and she really didn't want to impose any longer, they said their goodbyes and hugged at the door.

There were tears in her eyes as June wished her well.

Her shattered heart almost visible in her face, "Keep in touch, June. Goodbye dear."

The bus journey home seemed endless. *Life could be so tough,* she thought, *so testing.*

She longed to get home she wanted to cry, to be alone, to grieve for what might have been. Her heart was broken.

Walter was waiting for her at the bus stop, she could no longer hold back the tears.

"That's it, that's it. Let it all out," he held her close.

June was feeling a bit solemn for the few days that followed, if Mac had noticed he hadn't said anything, there was lots of stuff going round in her head.

Chapter Forty-Three

Memories, mostly nice ones of being with Matt, he could be funny at times, sad too when he'd talk about home, even angry but always caring.

She knew she'd done the right thing in letting him go, why did she always have to do the right thing! Why could she not have been selfish and asked him to stay, he might be alive today, they might have got married! Or not!

Goodness, there were a lot of memories flowing today, June thought, sitting by the sea listening to the ripple at water's edge had sent her thoughts back over all of her time with Matt. Was no wonder her head would spin sometimes with all that was going on inside it.

Walter came closer, "I say, wouldn't be sitting there too long now June," pointing up to the grey sky wasn't sure if June had heard him shout from the pier with the wind that was blowing.

"There's a storm a brewing."

He had startled her for a minute.

"You were away in another world there."

June smiled. Yes, she thought to herself, I was away in another world, if only.

She took Walter's arm as he hobbled along and together they walked in the wind. So much water under the bridge since she'd walked this way with Matt, yet the memories still so vivid.

The longing still real, the pain though now dulled still came like a wave over her from time to time, though the tears stop falling, the heart still weeps.

June stooped to pick up the letter on the hall floor, she recognised Clodagh's writing, she always did her J's with a kind of a squiggle.

She'd been taken ill with malaria, was to travel home within a couple of weeks when she was strong enough and wondered if it was asking too much of their friendship to ask if she could stay with June while recovering.

June had her letter in the next post reassuring her friend that it was perfectly okay to ask as much as she liked of their friendship, after all wasn't that what friends were for.

As she watched her get out of the taxi, June could see how very frail and sickly her friend looked. If this was her being stronger after a couple of weeks, what was she like when she had written that letter.

She was walking with a stick but smiling, as she walked up the garden path, June had to take a breath and hold her emotions so as not to let Clodagh see the pity in her face.

"It's so good to see you," Clodagh took June by the hand and stepped into the hallway, her hands were so cold.

"Come in, Come in. You're welcome. Sit down I'll make us some tea."

As she filled the kettle, June's hand was shaking,
Sickness, she thought.

Pop always said, "Your health is your wealth."

June used to think it was because they would never have known wealth in their lifetime and that was just something he would say to make them feel better, but there were no truer words.

The malaria had struck suddenly, it had weakened her so.

She would hope to fully recover and return to continue her work, her help was so badly needed.

June doubted that was going to happen any day soon, Clodagh was now the one needing help. She had fixed up Pop's old bedroom downstairs to make it handy for her, though Nan always said that was a cold old room but with the two hot water bottles in the bed and the new draught excluder on the front door, June hoped it would be nice and cosy for her.

The only thing now that worried her having seen her state was her having to climb the stairs to the bathroom, it was going to be difficult for her.

Chapter Forty-Four

They chatted for hours, it was like she hadn't had a chat in ages so June kept the kettle on the boil and the fire roaring and her friend talked to her heart's content.

"Clodagh's back," June thought she should tell Mac, be only a matter of time before someone would come in asking for her so she thought she might as well put him in the picture, he was very understanding and genuinely caring when he heard she hadn't been well, "She's lucky to have a friend like you, she'll be fine," Mac saw the concern in June's face.

As she got up from the breakfast table, Clodagh staggered. June reached out to help.

"Goodness, you'd think I was on the wobbly juice. It's the medication, makes me light-headed sometimes. I'm fine."

She walked with her stick to the sink holding on to every chair she passed for support, it was heart breaking.

"You know June, I'm feeling much stronger these days soon be out of your hair."

Clodagh smiled, there was a sadness in her eyes.

"You're welcome to stay as long as you like, don't be in any hurry," June walked towards her friend and hugged her, she could feel the bones in her back almost, she had gotten so thin. It was all she could do to stop herself from falling apart.

"I'll look after the cleaning up now, you be off. It's the least I can do to earn my keep. Go on off with you."

June couldn't argue, it was lovely to see her getting up and about but she worried that she wasn't able, she could see her struggle. Miles away, June had given Mrs Carey the wrong change,

"A penny for them."

"I'm so sorry Mrs Carey, late nights."

114

"Aw sure, yer only young once, you're grand."

She wasn't about to tell her she was out of her mind with worry, every waking moment she would be listening in case Clodagh was making her way up the stairs to the bathroom, and needed help.

Six weeks had passed, Clodagh was definitely getting stronger, June could see a big improvement especially in the last week. "I have booked my flight for the end of the week."

Clodagh seemed very pleased with herself.

"But are you sure you're only just getting your strength back," June wasn't sure it was a good idea, not yet.

"I'm good. Feel really well. Thank you June, don't know what I would have done without you these past few weeks, and as for Nan's chicken soup, goodness would bring you back from the dead. Think it probably did in fact," Clodagh laughed.

It was good to see her get her independence back, June would miss her.

Looking after her, cooking and making sure she had everything she needed gave her something to think about other than Matt and her own sad existence.

Mac was putting a sign in the window of the post office as June approached. "Got in a bit early, thought I'd get a good run at the day." Mac was full of the joys.

"Hi, Mac," June was carrying a holdall.

"You off somewhere nice?" Mac was also looking forward to the long weekend ahead.

"I am and I'm not, kinda between two minds," June wanted to talk to someone about the letter she had received the day before but was Mac the one to talk to, she wasn't sure.

Walter had brought it round, it was from Matt's mother, she hadn't had June's address so she had written to Walter and asked if he would pass the envelope enclosed in his letter to June.

Chapter Forty-Five

Seems Matt's friend Eric, who he had shared an apartment with him in America for his short stay had turned up on her doorstep, he had been so shattered after Matt's tragic death that he was no longer content to stay in America and had come home a couple of months after.

He had got to know him pretty well over that short time and wanted to pay his respects to his parents on his return.

Eric spoke of how Matt had such plans, he had confided in him about the situation at home and how he constantly worried about his mother, and he had told him about June.

"Guess she was kinda special," he'd said.

He'd handed Matt's mother a letter he had found in clearing up his own stuff to come home, "It must have slid under the cupboard, was sitting at the table with all my gear ready to go. Just taking it all in when I spotted the edge sticking out from under the cupboard."

It was addressed to June.

Matt's mother didn't want to open it so she had written to Walter to pass the letter on to June to ask if she would send her address and she would send it on or if she wanted to visit at any time she would be most welcome, most welcome indeed.

Reading between the lines, June thought a visit would be appropriate, it would be insensitive to just forward on her address and have the letter just sent on to her, maybe the last few lines her son had written, would be such a precious thing to his mother. She would visit.

It was a long weekend and she would take the bus and maybe spend some time.

But now with her hold-all packed and a B&B booked to stay overnight, June was wondering if it was the right thing to do, if only Clodagh was still there, someone to discuss this with.

"Mrs Sheridan was in, wondered if anyone had found keys, said I'd put a notice in the window, never know."

Mac climbed down from the window.

June left her holdall beside her desk and picked up the post. "So where are you off to? Somewhere nice I hope," he wiped down the chair he'd been standing on.

June knew he wasn't being nosey just showing an interest, it was early so she put the kettle on and they sat and talked for a while, she was glad she had discussed her situation with him, he was very understanding and it helped.

It was late when she checked into the B&B so June decided to wait until morning to go to visit Matt's mother.

She'd had a restless night twisting and turning, she wondered what would be in the letter. Probably all about his travels and all she was missing by not going with him, she thought.

Morning came with sunshine, June loved the spring.

The door was open as she approached Matt's house, she knocked and waited.

"Oh my goodness," Matt's mother had a towel in her hand as she came to the door.

"Come in my dear, I have the door open for a bit of fresh air, you know yourself when you have someone bedridden, toileting and all that. Sure they can't help it. Sit down I'll put the kettle on. It's good to see you."

She was just as Matt had described, fussing and fumbling around.

She remembered the softness in Matt's eyes as he spoke about his mother.

"There you are, I know it's hard. Sure you'd want to be made of stone. It's lovely to see you again, lovely."

As she handed June the letter, Matt's mother took a hankie out of her apron pocket and wiped her worn face of tears.

June's heart missed a beat as she saw Matt's handwriting, would she open it now or wait until she got back to the B&B. She opened the letter.

Chapter Forty-Six

My dear June, I have found a place to stay, sharing with another lad. We get on well and I have found a job. I hope things have worked out for you at the post office, I do miss you. I will always love you, be happy.

Matt xx

"I'm sorry," she knew this would happen, why did she open the letter, upsetting Matt's mother.

"That's okay dear, I know."

They sat in silence for a while and June asked how Matt's dad was, seems he had deteriorated further, slept a lot of the time now, it was lonely she said.

Ready for the road, June placed the letter safely in the side of her purse, there was a piece of paper already there, it was Valerie's phone number.

She checked out of the B&B and thanked the lady for the lovely comfortable stay, knowing she would never be back. "Good weekend?" Mac looked shattered.

"Okay and you?" The look was enough to tell it was a rough one.

Walter was the first customer, not in for any other reason, June thought, but to check to see if she was okay, such a sweetheart. "I'm doing shepherd's pie for dinner, will drop some over later," Walter seemed pleased to see she was okay.

"Thanks June, look forward to that," and he was off.

Mrs Sheridan had found her keys in the garden, as June walked home she called her to the gate, she reckoned the cat had taken them into the garden.

"Cheeky is right, the name suits him to the ground. Can't leave anything out of your hand but it's gone," she cuddled the cat affectionately as she spoke.

June had to laugh, "I'll tell Mac to take the sign out of the window then."

The shepherd's pie smelled delicious as she walked to Walter's house, she was starving and couldn't wait to get her feet off the ground.

Stuffed and feet up she fell into a deep sleep on the chair, everywhere was in darkness when she awoke, straight into bed clothes and all she was wrecked. She awoke in the early hours, Matt came into her thoughts, she jumped out of the bed to the wardrobe and took out the oil cloth covered sign that Matt had given her from the 'Mary Ellen' the smell brought back such memories. She cried herself back to sleep.

Walter had gone to join Lily, she had thought he looked tired the day before when she left him over the shepherd's pie but he seemed his usual self, grateful and cheery.

A passer-by had noticed the curtains were closed at lunchtime, which was very unusual, he had passed in his sleep in the very chair that Lily had passed away in her sleep a few years earlier. The guards were called and he was pronounced dead since the early hours, Mac had brought the news to June at the post office. It was a sad day. There would never be another Walter, she would never get to chat to him again about the old days and Lily. She had to console herself in knowing they were together again now, Lily was the love of his life. He had struggled to be without her these past few years. A letter was found on the mantelpiece, addressed to June.

He knew his time wasn't long and he wanted his wishes to be known should he pass suddenly.

June was in no state to comment as Father Mulcahy read the letter at the wake, she was heartbroken to lose her dear friend she never thought of life without Walter, nothing would ever be the same.

Chapter Forty-Seven

My dearest June, you were the daughter I never had.

Father Mulcahy went on to read Walter's letter:

If you are reading this letter, I have gone to be with my lovely Lily. I hope not to burden you but my solicitors name and details are enclosed. If you wouldn't mind, he has my will and last wishes. Of course, I will be buried alongside Lily, the love of my life. Be well my dear friend, you have been good to me.

June cried for days; she'd never felt so alone.

Walters's house had been locked up, a council house, soon there would be a new family there, all the memories the walls laced with photographs! All left behind.

Father Mulcahy came into the post office, "I saw you visit Walter's grave on Sunday. Goodness, it's hard to believe he's gone. He was like a part of the community you think would be there forever, ya know? June, I'm a long time wearing this collar and I've seen all sorts of tragedies, celebrations, you name it, but I will always remember the day Walter buried Lily."

He turned and walked away with tears in his eyes.

June had known Walter was lost without Lily and he was only biding his time, she'd stood at the graveside flowers still fresh, it was a cloudy day.

"One day at a time," she'd always remember Walter's old saying. "One day at a time."

As she walked on the beach, June thought to herself, it hadn't been that long since Walter had shouted to her that there was a storm brewing, they'd walked together up the pier that day. Mac had been very understanding in giving her time off, he didn't know Walter very well just had the odd chat with him, found him to be a very kind sort he had said.

Nancy came to the post office with her lovely daffodils,

"Must be a wedding today, Father Mulcahy is standing outside in his robes, don't hear of anyone getting married in these parts, did you June?"

June smiled to herself, she'd not heard of anyone getting married but she knew for sure Nancy wouldn't be long finding out!

"I see there's a man going round Walter's old place too, looks like an engineer maybe, he has a clipboard looking over the place. Poor Walter, not yet cold in the grave. That's life isn't it, girl."

As Nancy closed the door behind her, June couldn't hold back the tears, she'd lock up and go home, Mac was away on business, he wouldn't have minded anyway.

She walked past Walter's as usual on the way home, all cleared out now ready for the next tenants, as if he never existed. She would always remember Walter.

June wondered how Matt's mother was, she'd told herself she would never return there after her last visit but she had been on her mind now for a while, she would go to visit her.

Matt's dad was now totally bedridden. "Had to get home help in," his mother looked distraught as she sat opposite June clasping her frail little hands twisted with arthritis, "Another cup of tea?" her hand shook as she poured. Liam was a male nurse who called every morning to dress a bedsore on Matt's dad's back and the home help called at lunchtime and bedtime. "Don't know what I'd do without them, sure I'd never manage. Poor Matt, could do with him around now, the house is falling asunder."

June gave her the phone number of the post office and she was to ring if she ever needed to talk or ever needed anything.

Mac had organised a trip to visit his brother in America, June wasn't aware he'd had a brother, there was never any mention of it before.

Hearing the mention of the word America made her cringe. Lots of water under the bridge but still did something to her. "Sure I have a sister too, she's sort of the reason I am going. She's ill, very ill. Needs a kidney transplant. Thought I might have been able to donate but not compatible. Let's hope Pete can help, not exactly something to be discussed over the phone though."

Chapter Forty-Eight

No wonder, June thought, *Mac seemed away in a world of his own sometimes, no one knows what other people are going through*, she felt for him.

He'd be gone for ten days, hopefully come home with good news. June was just closing up, it had been a long week with Mac away and having to do the wholesalers herself she'd felt exhausted, the phone rang and she went back to her desk to answer it, Mac sounded very downhearted, his brother too was non compatible with his sister.

He would return with disappointment for his mother and his sister.

June reassured him that everything was going smoothly at her end and to try not to worry too much, she would have them in her prayers.

He was back and into the run of things again within the week, often sitting looking into space and looking shattered.

"Why don't you come to mine for a bit to eat tonight?" June wasn't sure it was the right thing to do but she felt he needed to talk and there was never ten minutes past without the door opening at the post office, was a busy little place, no time to talk.

"That would be nice, I'll bring the wine," Mac had a lovely smile, wasn't very often she saw it these days with all he'd had on his mind but it would melt butter.

Now, what would she cook, as she passed the eggs counter at the local grocery shop she thought of Matt.

It was as if another lifetime, Matt, Walter, Nan, Pop, Lily, time had a way of moving on even when you felt it stood still.

With the chicken roasting in the oven and the potatoes boiling away, June thought a quick shower and then put the vegetables on, it felt good to have company around again it had been a while.

"That hit the spot," Mac had cleaned his plate, "more wine," he topped up her glass and then his own, "To good friends and good cooks," they both laughed as their glasses touched.

"How did your sister take the news?" she had to ask.

"Aw sure, ever the hero my sister, took it okay. She won't give up hope, I don't know where to turn next, time is running out. She can't take another setback. Doctors don't know how she keeps going, she's amazing."

"I need to find out more about Roger Atkins, my mother came from round here. Married a man from these parts, Roger, he'd been carrying on with a local girl, was ripping off the business at the same time. Got her pregnant seemingly, did himself in, couldn't take the pressure apparently. She sold the family business and moved on, unaware that she too was pregnant with Roger, my sister is really my half-sister, my brother and I came along after her second marriage years later. We were only young when our dad was lost at sea. We did okay, Mam was great. Told you my life was complicated. If I could find out more about Roger and his lady friend, I might be able to get in touch with his other child, might be a match it's a long shot."

June felt sick, this was too much of a coincidence not to be connected, why hadn't the penny dropped, he had asked her ages ago if she'd known any Roger from around these parts, but she hadn't thought. Listening to Mac talk about his mother and her husband carrying on with a local girl and doing away with himself, ripping off the business, it all came together all of a sudden!

"Are you okay June?" Mac seemed concerned, "You look very pale."

"I'm fine, just tired I guess."

"How thoughtless of me," Mac got up to go.

"You've been holding the fort, you must be all tuckered out."

Chapter Forty Nine

With a friendly peck on the cheek and a big thank you for the lovely meal Mac was on his way oblivious to what was going through June's head.

It was an awful state of affairs altogether, none of her own doing but she was filled with guilt, shame, she wasn't sure what.

How could she face Mac again.

At the same time, how could she ignore the fact that she could be a match for Mac's sister, her half-sister too, it had just occurred to her.

She would offer to be tested for the donation of a kidney, Mac was shocked.

"You'd do that? For a complete stranger?"

"Well let's see first if it's a match, never know," and she wasn't sure if he could ever know the reason why, time would tell and at least if it wasn't a match she could lose the guilt, if it was well she would worry about that then!

Tests complete. June waited anxiously for the results, she hated hospitals, doctors and white coats, the lot. She wasn't sure how she would go through with it if she was a suitable candidate, this was a nightmare!

It all happened very quickly in the end, Mac went on to tell June how he'd gotten a call early that morning to say that his sister's condition had weakened and it was only a matter of hours, he was devastated.

She had passed peacefully, it was too little too late. June felt a sudden sadness.

She couldn't even grieve openly for her new found half-sister, didn't get the chance to offer her a chance to save her life, had the test proved her to be suitable, results of which she hadn't received yet and had no further interest in receiving now.

Didn't even get the chance to meet.

How would she continue to work beside Mac knowing now what she knew, it would be impossible.

As it happened, she didn't have to worry. Mac's mother wasn't coping very well and he had decided to sell up and move home, run the business for her.

He hoped to sell up as a going concern and assured June that her job would be safe, ever the gentleman, concerned about everybody. What would he say if he knew the truth about his loyal employee!

At least, now they would part on friendly terms, the issue could be avoided, he had no further interest in pursuing the Roger scenario!

The post office had changed hands yet again, June would go for dinner with Mac and meet her new employer, *A very fancy way of doing things,* she thought, but Mac always went out of his way to do things right.

A very pleasant looking elderly man sat with Mac as she entered the restaurant, Mac had picked her up but she had excused herself to go to the bathroom before she sat down, the man got up and shook her hand, a very firm handshake.

He was a businessman with a string of shops around the country, would be putting a manager in place and hoped that June would remain with them considering her experience, according to Mac, with both the business of running the post office and its clientele.

He would be delighted if she would stay.

June reassured him that she had no immediate plans to move on and would be delighted to keep her job there.

That sorted, they went on to have a lovely meal with really pleasant conversations, but June had been doing a lot of thinking throughout, she had become really good friends with Mac and would miss him terribly, and couldn't let him go not knowing that her results had come back to say that she was an ideal candidate for a transplant for his sister, and why.

She was going to tell him every gory detail of her past. She owed him that much. Sitting in his car outside her gate June told Mac her story, as much as she herself knew about her past, she'd never met nor heard anything about Roger Atkins, only that her mother had mentioned his name when she had asked her that day so long ago now, nor had her mother discussed her past with her on their short encounter, but she apologised for not telling him at the time she realised she was who he was looking for, she'd just panicked, she told him about her results and how she would have loved to have had a sister, she sympathised with him for his dreadful loss and she reached for the door.

"Wait," Mac put his hand over hers to stop her leaving the car. "Let's not part like this."

June looked at the tears rolling down his face,

"I did wonder, when you offered, but, just thought it would be too much of a coincidence. Goodness, what were the chances of that eh! Thanks for telling me June, I wish you well."

June opened her door with a shaking hand, she felt relief, but nothing could relieve her of the sadness she felt, for Mac's sister, for Mac, for herself, for all she had missed out on, and for Matt.

As she listened to the ring tone on the other side, June wasn't sure if she wanted to get an answer!

"Valerie, it's June."